LASSITER
2 RELOAD

by

ROBERT KING

Grosvenor House
Publishing Limited

This book is published by
Grosvenor House Publishing Ltd
Link House
140 The Broadway, Tolworth, Surrey, Kt6 7Ht.
www.grosvenorhousepublishing.co.uk

A CIP record for this book
is available from the British Library

ISBN 978-1-78623-805-4

About the author

Robert (Bob) King is now in his eightieth year and this is his second completed novel with yet still more future plans for the character 'Sam Lassiter'.

A multi faceted man who spends a majority of his time either painting or writing with a dash of singing too, along side this he is a volunteer at Poole Hospital Bookshop.

Dorset born and led a well travelled life, with scars and wrinkles to prove it, he then settled back in Dorset in the beautiful town area of Poole and has a daughter, two sons and five grandchildren.

Acknowledgements

I would like to thank four wonderful friends for their support and input into Lassiter II 'Reload'.

Alison (Ali) Martin, Drew Illman, Sharon Jaques and Steve Hunt

Whose help, encouragement and support made it possible for me to complete my second novel, spurring me on to start my third!

Chapter 1

Sam Lassiter sat in the lounge aboard his luxury cruiser the "John Jo" on a hot Sunday afternoon in mid July 1955. It had been a year since the bringing down of the Russian Mafia in Catalina.

He was happy with his own company now and although it was only just over a year since the passing of Janet he was starting to come to terms with it and getting some kind of closure. He did realize however that this would never be a complete closure.

So, he had a wonderful home here on the water, a Ferrari Monza Spider, a regular well paid job with Doctor John Li commuting between LA and New York City and a retainer from Washington DC. Financially he was in good shape. He had also the beautiful California climate.

A surprize cable arrived a few weeks later from General Boyd-Richards, it read:

Dear Sam,

You were never much of an incentives person, so I didn't mention anything prior to the Catalina Operation. But any monies received in the Government account would be subject to a bonus to you of 1% of the total monies received. Therefore 1% of Nine Hundred and Seventy Million Dollars is $9.74 Million Dollars. This amount has been transferred to your account in First National Bank in Santa Barbara. I have arranged for the National Lottery people to send the cheque to the bank for this amount so that you don't have to pay any Tax.

Most of the missions received from the Pentagon during 1955 were pretty routine stuff, body guarding Politicians and VIPs,

So Sam's itinerary was well established, 4 weeks in California and 4 weeks in New York City, bouncing between the two clinics of John Li's. This schedule tied in very nicely as he could link up with his friends Chris and Mary Jo from Precinct 52 and also enable him to drive down to DC and touch base with General Boyd-Richards who was always pleased to see him.

Sam back in his lounge aboard the "John Jo" was busy writing to his friends in the UK when the telephone rang.

'Hi it's Monique,'

'Hi "Spud", said Sam,

'I have an invitation for two to attend the Premier of the new Glenn Ford movie at the LA Hilton on Saturday next. Can you be my escort for the evening as Colin has to go to New York where my brother has staff problems,'

'Of course I will stand in for him it will be good to get the old tuxedo out of wraps,' said Sam.

'It's good PR for me to mix with the stars, good for business,' she said.

The hired Limo pulled up adjacent to the red carpet and Monique eased her way out showing the majority of her long sun tanned legs. Sam took her hand and guided her along the carpet which was surrounded on both sides by a mass of photographers. The photographers were all over Monique who looked stunning in a low cut white Dior number, the skirt split on one side from the floor to her waist.

As the movie got underway Sam noticed the leading lady.

'Well I'm buggered,'he said,

'What,' said Monique,

'That girl there, the leading lady Desiree de Carlo,'

'What about her,' said Monique.

'I lived with her for over a year in a tent in Korea, that's Sergeant Desi Carpenter,' said Sam.

The film premier ended to be greeted by a crescendo of applause. All the audience adjourned to the enormous lounge area where drinks and delicate snacks were served. The actors, actresses, producers and directors all did there circulating thing and making sure that the photographers shot there best side. Desiree De Carlo was within a couple of yards of Sam and Monique, Desiree looked over her shoulder staring into space looking totally bored with the whole thing and not really wanting to be there.

Sam called out 'Sergeant Carpenter front and centre', Desiree looked around and saw Sam and with a huge smile on her face said,

'Sergeant Carpenter reporting for duty Sarge,'

She came over to Sam and gave him a huge hug and a peck on the cheek.

'It is so good to see you Sam,'

'It was such a surprise to see you on the big screen, I had no idea,' said Sam.

'I see you are still as beautiful as ever,' he said.

'We need to spend some time together Sam and talk about everything that has happened in the last few years,' she said.

'Here's my card, call me and you can buy me dinner,' she said laughing.

'I'll leave you to get on with what you are supposed to do Des, I'll give you a call,' said Sam.

As Monique and Sam departed the Hilton Hotel Monique turned to Sam and said 'I can't believe you know Miss De Carlo',

'Neither can I.' said Sam.

The next day Sam phoned Desi and left a message on her answer phone to the effect that he would be in New York for four weeks and would telephone her on his return to Santa Barbara.

Sam then called Sergeant Christine Stacey and Detective Mary Jo Bonetti and arranged to go to dinner with them at Dempsey's in Time Square.

Sam flew into New York on the Friday and settled himself in at the penthouse on 5th Avenue. He took a shower which brought back wonderful but sad memories of Janet and her short stay in Manhattan. Sam put on a track suit and chilled in front of the TV.

He then phoned Christine at her home to confirm the dinner arrangements for Saturday at Dempsey's.

It was great to see the girls again they had become more than just working partners they were trusted and good friends. Sam talked about his life in California, his work and the still problem of getting any closer to closure on the loss of Janet. Chris said that she and David were trying for a baby and Mary Jo talked about her kids one of which the lad Harry was thinking seriously of joining the Marines.

'So hows the crime in the big City," said Sam.

'Pretty box standard apart from one really nasty case,' said Chris.

'We have a paedophile who is calling the "rent boy" agencies, taking a kid to a hotel and doing what these animals do to the kids and then he films them while he kills them. The new speak on the block is "Snuff" killing.'

'Look I'm working all day on Monday, but I'm free on Tuesday afternoon, why don't I come to the 52nd and try to work a profile on this bastard,' said Sam.

'Do you both remember I was working on the ultimate Profiling Package well it's as good as it's going to get, I've put together the package using the excellent work from the top agencies worldwide and pieced it together within my brief. So the complete package has input from the FBI, CIA, MI5, LAPD, London MET and Interpol,' said Sam.

'Ok Sam Tuesday it is I'll run it across the Captain.'

Sam spent the Sunday doing his washing and ironing and writing letters to Colour Sergeant Len Jackson and Trisha at Camberley. On the Monday two breast enhancement operations and one nose job were carried out in the New York clinic. He arrived back at the Penthouse early evening took a shower and popped a lasagne in the oven, then settled down to watch some TV.

Tuesday morning he spent servicing the anaesthesia equipment and generally cleaning the OR at the clinic. After lunch he took the Metro across town to the Bronx and the 52nd Precinct.

Chapter 2

Sam's welcome at the 52nd was like the prodigal son returning, hugs and handshakes all round. Chris had secured a conference room for the get together. Four additional Detectives plus the newly appointed Captain Steve Fletcher. Sam produced his profile manual and started the long question and answer process. After 6 hours of deliberation Sam called a halt.

'Ok here's what I've got,' said Sam.

Sam laid out all the options of the situation as it stood. These are the things that need to be put in place and put to bed soonest:

1) 'Check on all the escort services in the New York area, whether female, male and see if rent boys are on the menu,'
2) 'I believe the perp is a person of high intelligence a Doctor, Lawyer or Politician or another professional.'
3) 'I can take care of all the thousands of Doctors in the area as far as there medical records go. I'm looking for HIV here.'
4) 'Check all the doctors wives or girlfriends for the virus.'

5) 'Get as many rent boys examined as possible for sexually transmitted diseases,'
6) 'Get as many phone taps on Escort Agencies as we can,'
7) 'Check if any Doctor's, Surgeon's are receiving treatment for HIV or AIDS,'
8) 'I think this guy and maybe his partner are on the way out with AIDS and they are going to take as many people who they hold responsible with them,'

We know that the last "snuff" kill, that the lad was carrying the HIV virus, so our man may well have attracted the disease and at the risk of repeating myself check the hospitals for any of the Doctors menfolk receiving testing for HIV.

'Lets get together in 1 week and review the situation, if that's ok with you Captain?' Said Sam.

'Lets do it people, Chris you take point on this I'll give you as much help as I can,' said the Captain.

'Ok to summarize, the bottom line then guys is I believe that the perp is a Doctor or Physician of some sort, highly intelligent, a homosexual with a pension for young boys. I believe also that it is payback time snuffing out the young people that transmitted the virus to him, i.e. the rent boys,'

Sam returned to the Penthouse on 5th and made the phone call to Virginia.

'Don't you ever go home sir,' said Sam.

'Too many bad people out there Colonel Lassiter,' said the General.

'Quite a task for your team at the Pentagon sir, I need to know if any Doctors, Surgeons, Senators or high ranking officials in the New York area are HIV positive,' said Sam.

'We have ways and means of bursting through red tape as far as patient confidentiality is concerned, I'll get right on it Sam.'

Sam phoned Chris to inform her that his people at the Pentagon had taken up the Doctor medical search and that she could release her team members from that task and start the surveillance on some prominent players.

'I've got something for you to Sam, Detective Penny Carter has the ear of a local pimp who informed her that he had some information, if the price was right.'

'Tell Penny to set up a meet with the guy and if the info is kosher, he'll get his money.' said Sam.

Sam met the slimy guy at a deserted diner in Brooklyn and he sang like a canary. Sam said he would check it out and if it proved reliable he would get his money.

Sam mobilised a phone trace team and placed the call.

'Good morning Gaytime Escort Agency,' how can I help you', a female voice said.

'Good morning I would like to book six young lads to entertain at a Gentlemen's Party,' said Sam.

'Can I ask who gave you this number sir,' said a male voice.

'You can ask but that information must remain confidential,' said Sam.

'If you cannot accept this I'm afraid we will not be doing any business,' Sam continued.

'Did he give you any idea who he was', the man said.

'Not really only some stupid reference to a Disney character,' said Sam.

'Ah yes, when and where Sir, the cost will be $5000,' said the male voice.

'The money is not a problem, I do however require the utmost secrecy and confidentiality,' said Sam.

'You have that guarantee sir,' 'i'll talk to my people and get back to you later today.' said Sam replacing the phone in sync with the phone call tracer.

'2024 Harbour Heights and 2nd Avenue, lower Manhattan, lets go, get some officers there pronto and break the door down if we have to,' said Sam.

'Confirmation we have a warrant to break and enter.' said Mary Jo.

A large burly cop built like a Linebacker smashed the door off it's hinges and everybody charged in. 'Nobody move, Police,' yelled Chris.

'Read them there rights Mary Jo and take e'm down town and lock them up.' said Chris.

Fortunately they didn't have time to destroy all the incriminating evidence. Sam and the two girls waded through it all.

'Ok we have a Mr. Pluto, Mr. Goofy, Mr. Donald and a Mr. Grumpy they seem to be the principal players, at least the ones who are spending the big money,' said Sam.

'Lets bring them in, I'll have some Doctor's standing by to run HIV tests on all of them, there wives, girl-friends or boyfriends we need to check for any traces of the virus.' satd Chris.

The addresses established and searches were made at 2am. Precinct 52 personnel struck gold. Doctor Raymond Livingstone aka Mr. Pluto, the top Surgeon at Montefiore Medical Centre was arrested. Pictures of young boys littered his study along with "Snuff" movies with him taking the staring role. When the good Doctor was questioned by Sergeant Chris Stacey he broke down in tears and confessed.

'You will remain in custody until your trial date, no bail will be granted, you will be charged with Murder 1,' said Chris.

Sergeant Chris Stacey addressing the crowded Detective Room at the 52nd, said, 'That the child sex circle had been smashed and all the main players charged with sex with juveniles and participation in "Snuff" movies, all murder 1.'

Sam watched all this on channel 9 News from the comfort of the lounge at the Penthouse. He hoped the perpetrators would proven guilty and sent to death row.

Early the following morning Chris phoned her thanks to Sam for his massive input on the case and said that she had received a promotion to Lieutenant and Mary Jo to Sergeant.

'Congratulations to you both, you're good cops,' said Sam.

The "Snuff" team hierarchy was demolished with arrests being made in New Jersey, Carolina, Memphis and Florida with all perpetrators arrested and charged with serious sex offences.

One week later prior to his first court hearing Doctor R. Livingstone was found hanging from a leather belt around his neck in his cell.

Sam returned to his duties at the New York clinic for the next two weeks before departing once more for LA.

Chapter 3

When Sam arrived back on board he had two letters waiting for him from the UK, one from Katherine and one from Len Jackson. He opened Katherine's letter, she wrote: I seem to be the bearer of bad news every time I write to you Sam, but somebody this side of the water has got to do it. Trisha's husband has been to hospital for what he thought was routine blood tests, it appears it's not so routine, he has been diagnosed with a rare blood disorder akin to leukaemia. It can be treated but not cured the Specialist said. Trisha has quit her job at the Officer's school and is nursing Trevor around the clock.

I've been trying to help out with some cash but typical Trisha she refuses to take it. Things must be tight with them Sam as Trisha is looking after him full time.

Sam replied immediately to Katherine's letter and asked for her bank details. He said that he would deposit some pennies in her account and you will have to find Trish and Trevor's account details by fair means or foul. She must not be told where the money is coming from. I'll be over for my 6 weeks holiday soon and we'll catch up. He received Katherine's bank details by return and placed $20000 in her account for Trisha and family.

'If you have problems with Trishia with regard to the money, then go directly to the top man for this kind of illness and hire him.' said Sam,

Chapter 4

Sam was enjoying the long sunny California days and was happy with his own company. Jill had left the area and returned to work in Wisconsin and Sandra was transferred to the FBI headquarters in Quantico Virginia. He was doing things he had never done before, boat rides and a bit of fishing. He cleaned both boats until they were gleaming and carried out some basic maintenance. He turned the giant engines over, checked the Navigation gear and the ship to shore radio.

Sam took the little boat out for a day trip and a bit of fishing and dropped anchor in the same area as a bunch of other craft. He was reading the local newspaper when the lead story jumped off the page. There was a picture of a middle aged woman with a boob job that went severely wrong. Swelling, bruising, lop sided, nipple hardening and lips like a pouting gold fish. 'This is what they did to me,' she quoted. A few new Cosmetic Surgery clinic's have opened in the LA area recently smelling the big bucks, they were however "Cowboys" and shouldn't be allowed anywhere near a scalpel. Unfortunately these clinics are still operational the article went on to say.

Sam wrote to Doctor John Li.

Hi John.

I'm certainly not really qualified in suggesting this, but as a member of the Board of Doc Li's Clinic's I think it is my duty to do so. These "Cowboy" clinics are popping up all over LA and are giving out the wrong message with bungling methods and ruining a lot of women's lives. I will take care of these idiots.

I think its time to review and improve our after surgery care procedures so that we are air tight. A letter from you to the FDA (Food and Drug Administration) suggesting additional research into the manufacture of Silicone and Saline implants is required. I believe after care service is more important than the actual operations.

Signed Sam.

Doctor John's response was immediate and he placed a Surgeon in every after surgery care session. During the next few weeks Sam targeted all the "Cowboy" cosmetic surgery outfits in the Los Angeles area and paid them a visit, under the premise that his wife was too embarrassed to attend.

Twelve of these Clinic's were checked out by Sam and only 7 were complying with FDA rules and regulations. Leaflets were produced saying loud and clear that these outfits should be closed down due to incompetent surgery and back up facilities.

Small high explosive devices were placed in position and the detonation set for 3am, this would prevent any injuries to third party's. Within a week of the bomb attacks the targeted businesses closed or moved to another location.

The leaflets did the trick again as the Police Officer investigating said that it was probably a Women's liberation Group that had hired some hit men to plant the explosives.

Chapter 5

July arrived and Sam started on his yearly holiday in the UK to meet his old friends. He had written to Lance about his forthcoming visit and Lance had insisted that he stay at Sunningdale Manor. Lance had also set up some lectures for Sam at Camberley, Lympstone and the Commando School at Bickleigh. The Commanding Officers in each Division were more than happy to have a VC address there troops. Incidently you can pick up a nice cheque for your services as you are now a civilian.

Sam landed safe and sound in London, then took a Greenline bus to Camberley and then a cab up to the Manor. He was greeted by a bear hug from Lance and his wife who introduced there little girl called Emma. They all sat down on the terrace and were served tea. The Templeton's talked Sam through all the things that had occurred during the last year and Sam relayed his year in the States.

Lance said the grass cutting of the 40 acres of land was going slowly as some of his cutters had been taken ill with a flu virus.

'I can cut grass, let me help Lance,' Sam sat astride one of the giant grass cutting mowers and after a brief instruction period was ready to go. The grass was cut and left for the gatherer to collect batch and bind, this done the trailers were loaded and shipped off to the winter feed manufacturer's. Sam loved being out in the open air working with the team of cutters. He made friends quickly and was invited to a nine pin bowling night at the local pub. Lance joined the bowling party and it was obvious to Sam that the workers were at one with Lance. Sam and Lance had to much to drink and were both quietly pissed.

'Better leave the car here,' said Lance,

'My cab awaits you sir,' said Sam, pointing to an old tractor in the corner of the Car Park.

They were travelling back to the Manor in the tractor, Sam driving and Lance hanging on for dear life, they were using the back roads before entering one of the recently cut fields of the Sunningdale Estate. Sam drove right up to the front steps that lead to the main entrants and came to a shuddering halt.

They both came round at 6am in the Manor's kitchen, neither of them knowing whether it was Christmas or New Years Eve. Lance slowly made his way to his bedroom and Sam took a shower and left for the stables to collect his mower. He worked with the cutters for a whole week until the last field was completed.

Chapter 6

Before departing for Camberley for his first session of lectures using Lance's 1953 Allard K3 Roadster.

Lance turned towards them both and said,

'Why don't you both go down to Trisha's you could both help out for a few days and give Trish a bit of a breather,'

'Bloody good idea Lance as long as she's ok with it, said Katherine.

'Ok see you both at dinner that's 7pm,' said Lance.

'See you later guys, I'm off for a run.' Said Sam .

Sam set out at a steady pace across the vast Sunningdale Manor Estate, he pounded out the first couple of miles, then briefly stopped at the top of a brow. He looked into the distance and saw Katherine thundering along full gallop on her beloved Soloman. He returned to the Manor House on what must have been a 5 mile run, went to his room, showered and changed into a track suit. He met Katherine in the lounge who was nursing a large martini.

'Would you like a drink Sam,' she said.

'A glass of water would be nice and shove some ice in it please,' said Sam. They sat down together on a large four seater sofa and Katherine said,

'You are still having problems Sam, you still haven't got over it have you,' she said.

'It's been over a year since the accident but I'm still having problems dealing with it', said Sam.

'I really couldn't express myself on the phone or by letter but we really did love each other Katherine,' said Sam.

'I know you were both very much in love, I know Mommy was and I was so happy for her,' said Katherine.

Dinner passed with the whole Templeton family together, it was wonderful thought Sam to see a family so bonded together. The children behaved beautifully with impeccable table manners.

'Ok good night folks see you at breakfast', said Sam,

Chapter 7

They were on the road to Camberley at 9am the big Allard cruising along at a steady 80 miles an hour,

'Do you think she has any idea where the money came from,' said Sam,

'I haven't told her but she's a cute cooky she'll probably work it out,' said Katherine.

They were greeted by a beautiful but sad faced Trisha who hugged them both as If there was no tomorrow, tears streaming down her face.

'I'm sorry ', she said as she led them to Trevor who was sitting in a wheel chair with a blanket over his knees. He was looking tired and very weak but managed a big smile when he saw the pair of them. Katherine and Trisha left for the kitchen and women's talk and Sam stayed and talked to Trevor who talked quite openly about his illness. Sam gave Trevor a brief resume of his life in California. Trisha looked at Katherine with those sad blue eyes and said,

'The money that you passed on to me went towards bringing in the top specialist who has been looking after Trevor these past few months. He told me yesterday that they have been unable to stop the spread of the cancer and at best Trevor has is 6 months to live,'

'Shit I'm so sorry Trish,' said Katherine.

'I'm going to give him all the love and affection until he passes,'

'I know you will.' said Katherine. The two girls returned to the living room to find Trevor and Sam staring in earnest at a chess board.

'He's creaming me, said Sam.

For the first time in a few months Trevor had a wide smile on his face.

'If it's ok with you Trisha we would like to go to the nursery school and pick up young Thomas', said Sam,

'Great idea', said Trisha.

After Trisha had put Trevor to bed, the three of them sat in the lounge Trisha looked at Sam and said,

'The cash we received from Katherine was used to engage the finest physician in England to try and sort out Trevor's problem and last evening said that he was so sorry but his statement last week that Trevor would have around six months to live is not correct he said expect to move Trevor into a Hospice sooner rather than later. He was unable to stop the spread of the cancer.

Said that he could not stop the cancer spreading and gave Trevor a matter 0f weeks rather than months..

'I really don't know what to say, sorry doesn't seem to cut it,' said Sam.

'If it wasn't for the money we received from you, Trevor would be no longer with us,' said Trisha.

'It wasn't charity it was to two people that I love dearly.' said Sam.

The long protracted silence was broken by Trisha who said 'There's nothing to say is there,'

'Not really it's so sad,' said Katherine.

The next three days Katherine and Trisha spent cleaning, washing and cooking while Sam took David out for a spin in the Allard or pushing him around in his chair and every afternoon picked up Thomas from Nursery school.

'I've got a couple of speaking engagements so i'll have to leave tomorrow,' said Sam.

'I'll stay until the weekend if I may Trish,' Said Katherine.

'You can stay as long as you like hon.' said Trisha.

Trisha and Katherine returned to the kitchen to prepare the evening meal while Sam played with young Thomas with Trevor looking on.

'Time for bed Thomas,' Trisha called from the kitchen,

'I want Uncle Sam to put me to bed,' said the little lad,

'No problem get up those stairs,' said Sam laughing,

After putting Thomas to bed Sam returned to the lounge.

'Sam I'm not going to make it you know,' said Trevor,

'Bollocks the specialist said that you are on the mend,' said Sam.'

'You are a wonderful friend Sam but a bloody awful liar', said Trevor,

'It hurts like hell and I'm taking far to many pain killers, I would really like to go quickly,' said Trevor

'I know that you live miles away in the US but if you could keep in touch with Trish she would love it and so would I,' said Trevor.

'That's a promise Trevor,' said Sam.

'The Templeton's are a wonderful family and will keep a special eye on Trisha making sure that she is ok.' said Sam.

The next day Sam said farewell to Camberwell and set out for Lympstone for the first of two lectures, dropping off Katherine at Camberley centre so she could do some shopping. So a sad Sam rolled into Lympstone for his talk to the young Marine recruits. Sam used the same format for all his little talks opening it up as soon as possible for questions from the floor. A lovely surprise greeted Sam as he climbed the steps to the stage, there sitting on the stage were his old mentor General Farquason – Keith and the now recently retired Colour Sergeant Crook.

'Firstly' Sam began 'What a great surprise having two old friends up here on stage with me, this is General Farquason – Keith he to blame for getting me a commission in the Corps. The other gentle man is Colour Sergeant Crook my old Troop instructor. The session was a great success with a superb reaction from the young Marines attending.

'Finally gentlemen one thing I want you to remember when you go on active service and that is: When you are on a mission everybody in and everybody out, don't leave anybody behind.'

Sam stood to accept the applause and asked the General and Colour Sergeant to come and stand next to him. Sam went along to the Officer's Mess for a brief chat before setting off for the Commando School at Bickleigh.

CHAPTER 8

He arrived at Bickleigh at 7pm and was immediately handed a telegram by the duty Corporal, it was from Katherine, it said:

> Hi Sam, Trevor had a bad day today and has been taken into Intensive Care at Camberley General. Kate.

'Can I send a telegram from here Corporal', said Sam.
'Not a problem Sir, I'll see to it'.

> Hi Katherine, I have this lecture to give tomorrow, will be with you guys early Saturday morning. Sam

He went directly to the mess and met the Commanding Officer, some other Officers and some NCO Instructor's.

'Colour Sergeant Jackson seems to be missing sir,' said Sam,

'Here he is now,' said the Colonel.

Len Jackson appeared as a fully fledged Captain, 'I don't believe I'm seeing this,' said Sam.

'Did the sums Colonel Lassiter and as I'm up for retirement next year an Officer's pension looks good to me.' said Len.

The lecture went ahead following Sam's normal pattern getting questions from the floor, with Captain Jackson chipping in where necessary.

'One final point I would like to make, things aren't looking to good in the middle and far east at the moment and you could well be called into action, remember not all of you guys are going to be awarded your green beret's, some of you will drop out and some will be back squaded. So whether you are a ship Marine or a Commando remember that you are a part of the finest fighting force in the world. Thank you so much for your participation today and if and when you get into action, good hunting.' Said Sam sitting down to a rousing reception.

In the Mess afterwards Sam turned to the Colonel and said 'I have a friend who is in a bad way in the Intensive Care Unit in Camberley and I have to get back there ASAP, keep in touch Captain Jackson', Sam said with a smile.

Sam gave the Allard a good clearing out on the way back to Camberley keeping the speed over 80 for the entire trip. He arrived late on the Friday evening and went directly to the Intensive care Unit. Trevor was lying in a bed with all sorts of tubes attached to him, looking very pale and very small like he was wasting away. He had a mask over his mouth and nose a constant supply of air being fed into him. Sam settled down in a chair by the side of Trevor's bed and prepared for a long nights vigil. Three hours later he was woken up by a Nurse.

'I'm sorry sir Mr. Jeavon's has been taken to theatre, it's an emergency situation, his wife has been informed.

Sam sat alone in the Cafeteria drinking an awful cup of coffee waiting for news on Trevor and waiting for Trisha to arrive. After 20 minutes had passed Trisha and Katherine arrived and the three of us waited anxiously for news on Trevor. The time went slowly with all three of them drinking as much coffee as possible to keep awake. Sam stood up and stretched his legs and walked over to the notice board and browsed through the contents. At 3am a tired looking Surgeon appeared and went directly to Trisha, 'I'm sorry Mrs. Jeavon's Trevor didn't make it, the cancer had spread to his lungs and we could not save him.' he said.

Trisha and Katherine broke down completely tears flooding down there cheeks, Sam held them both in a consoling bear hug. Trevor's body was taken to the morgue later and then on to the Funeral Directors. The funeral was scheduled for the following Tuesday.

The church was overflowing for Trevor's funeral with relatives and friends attending. Lance and his family were there along with many Officer's from the Camberley Campus.

As Sam was leaving Trisha came over to him and wished him a safe flight. Sam said that he would come over at Christmas and come and see her and her son. Sam left the funeral gathering for the airport satisfied that Lance and Katherine could look after Trisha.

He landed at New York Idlewild Airport and then took a cab to Manhattan. He was pleased that Doctor John had heeded his warning on the after surgery counselling and was making a concious effort to ensure patient satisfaction. Sam completed the 4 week programme at the clinic before leaving once more for LA.

CHAPTER 9

He arrived in LA late afternoon, took the Greyhound to Santa Barbara and then a cab to the Marina, where he settled down and caught up with his mail. He turned on the TV and watched some American Football. He thought how strange it was that they called it football as 99% of the time the ball was in hand.

Eva who was a Mexican lady was Sam's cleaner and was busy polishing away as though there was no tomorrow.

'Hey Eva take a break, sit down and have a coffee,'

'You are a very different boss man Mr. Sam, no other people that I work for would make such an offer.'

'Come and sit down for 5 minutes and take a break,' said Sam.

'How's the family,' he continued.

Eva broke down and a few tears ran down her face.

'Manalito my 10 year old is in trouble with the Police, he mix with bad company, do crimes, vandalism and do dope, also cause problems in harassing old people and stealing there money. We live in bad area of Santa Barbara called San Rouge near Goleta North, trouble everywhere,' she said.

'The Police are holding him,' said Eva.

'Ok, get your coat on lets go to the "Nick",' said Sam.

'What is Nick.' she said.

'The Police Station.' said Sam.

As they drove through the streets of Goleto Sam could see why there was so much crime in the area, Lots of youths walking the streets in gangs, Mexicans, Peurto Ricans, Blacks, all looking for trouble. They arrived at the Police Station and approached the desk Sergeant.

'The kid is being released no charges, he was just in the wrong place when the arrests went down, just a bystander.' He made a call and Manalito came out head bowed and hugged his Mother.

'Sorry Mama' he said. Sam confronted the desk Sergeant and said 'Is there any youth clubs that these kids can go to and get them off of the streets,'

'They would probably beat the shit out of the place, what they need is a outside facility more like a boot camp.'

Sam, Eva and the kid left the Station and although a group of young guys were hanging around his Ferarri it didn't seem to be damaged.

'Nice wheels,' said a tall slim black guy.

'Yes she is, I'll be coming back into this area soon, and I'll make a point of giving you a ride,' said Sam.

'That would be cool,' said the young man.

'You can buy it off me if you like, it will cost you 400,' said Sam.

'400 dollars,'

'400 thousand dollars,' said Sam.

'I'll pass said the young guy as he wandered away through the badly lit streets of down town Goleta.

Sam said his good byes to Eva and her son and drove through the poorly lit streets of Gorleta. He passed by an old basketball court that was in need of a good makeover, weeds coming through the surface of the playing area and the whole court covered in grafiti.

The next morning while Eva was hoovering the carpets in the upper deck lounge Sam asked if Manalito and any of his friends played soccer. 'They love to play but nowhere but the streets to kick around in,'

'There is a disused basketball court on 3rd Avenue and Jackson get Manalito and his friends along at 4pm next Tuesday.' said Sam.

CHAPTER 10

Sam made the phone call to the local Police at Goleta and talked with the top man at this sub-station.

'We've got to try and get these kids off the street Captain' said Sam and poured out his ideas. A disused basketball court on 3rd and Jackson would be a start where I could teach basic soccer skills to the young Mexican kids,'

'You have my permission to use the court, it is in fact owned by the Santa Barbara Police Department and as you know only 100 yards from our Precinct,' said the Captain.

'What I will do is get my mobile teams to pass by the court during there shift, in case you have any unwanted visitors,'

'Thank you so much sir, I will be starting coaching Tuesdays and Thursdays 4pm till 6pm.' Said Sam replacing the phone.

Tuesday arrived and Sam in his track suit viewed the 8 young Mexican kids that had turned up. Four young Latino's stood at the gate wondering what was going on. Sam assembled the whole group in a circle and said.

'Does everybody understand English,' and all the lads nodded a yes.

'The Goleta Juniors Football Club has only 2 rules, enjoy yourself and no race discrimination, we are all players no "wet backs", no "spics" no "niggers" and no "honkies", Are we clear,' said Sam.

'We just want to play ball,' said a little Mexican lad.

'Ok lets go,' Control, Passing, Tackling Sam ran through the session thoroughly enjoying himself. But most of all the lads were enjoying themselves as well. 'Ok last ten minutes 4 a side, lets see what you have got.' Sam finally blew his whistle and said 'Well done guys very impressive, get home safe and I'll see you all on Thursday 4pm, and bring a note from your folks saying that you have permission to attend.'

As Sam was leaving the court two young men stood directly in his path preventing him from leaving the court.

'What the fuck do you thing you are doing,' said a slick looking Peurto Rican.

'I'm trying to get some young lads off the streets and away from trash like yourself, now unless you want to spend a night in intensive care, I suggest you get out of my way,' Sam pushed pass the two Latino's. As he brushed passed the two yobs he heard the tell tell noise of a blade being released from a flick knife, he paused for a split second, spun on his left leg and launched a reverse kick with his right leg towards the knife carrier, which caught him square on the jaw. The lad was out before he hit the ground. A Police mobile unit was passing by and witnessed the whole incident, and radioed for an ambulance to tend to the injured teenager.

'Sam said his good byes to the young lads reminding them to be on time on Thursday and to tell there friends to come along.

Sam was just leaving the down town area of Goleta when he saw a sign which read Goleta Junior High School, he slowed down and saw a young women just about to get into her car. He drove up along side her vehicle and said,

'Excuse me Miss are you a teacher here,'

'Who wants to know,' she said.

'My name is Sam Lassiter and I've just finished a soccer training session with some of your pupils, we are using an old Basketball court in South Gorleta. There is a need to get these kids off the streets and away from the drug pushers,' said Sam

'I agree Mr. Lassiter make an appointment to come and discuss it with me, my name is Sharon Clark I'm the Principal here at Goleta Junior High.'

'Thanks Miss Clark I'll call you tomorrow.' said Sam slipping easily into his Ferarri.

CHAPTER 11

As Sam returned to the Marina he spotted the over-grown sports field at Goleta Junior High, we can do something with that thought Sam.

The following morning Sam had to assist in one boob job and one nose job, in the afternoon another breast enhancement.

As soon as these were completed he got on the phone to Ms. Clark

'Good afternoon Mr. Lassiter,'

'Afternoon to you Ma'am,' said Sam,

'I have a proposal for you,' he continued,

'I'll get the top field mowed and marked out, get the goal posts and crossbars fabricated, get the nets made and with a bit of luck get football shirts, shorts, socks, boots and pads, all free of charge via a sponsor,'

'If you allow me to teach soccer skills every Tuesday and Thursday at 4pm, then we are good to go,'

'Bring your training schedules in for me to have a look at and I'm sure we can get this thing going,' said Ms. Clark.

'You are right Mr. Lassiter it would be nice to get these young boys off the streets.'

Sam replaced the phone and immediately dialed Doctor Li

'I need Manuel for a couple of hours with his gang mowers to cut the grass at Goleta Junior Highs sports field, what's the chances Jon,' said Sam,

'Not a problem call Manuel and say I've said ok.'

'That's great, thanks Jon.'

Sam arrived at the old basketball court 5 minutes ahead of schedule with a bag of balls and some road cones, To his surprise 22 young lads were there waiting for him.

Sam lined them up in two teams of 11 and set out the cones, he said 'This is what I want you to do,' He proceeded to dribble with the ball in and out of the cones. 'It's called ball control,' said Sam. The session continued with shooting and passing techniques and a final free for all 10 minutes match.

'Good session lads, I'll let Manuel know where we will be next Tuesday, we could be at a new place, I'll be in touch.' said Sam.

Sharon Clark had a PTA meeting at 4pm on the Friday, Sam was in attendance and sat at the rear of the Gym. Sam took a close look at Sharon Clark, she was about 5 foot 6, blonde hair, good athletic figure and was nicely tanned. He was looking for the response from the parents regarding his soccer training sessions. 'Finally before you have a chat with the various teachers about your children, you probably noticed that the top playing field has been beautifully cut and manicured, this is due to a request from an Englishman to teach our young boys soccer skills. At this point in time it would be Tuesdays and Thursdays 4pm to 6pm, what is the general opinions from you all,' said Ms. Clark.

Eva Rodregez Sam's cleaner put her hand up.

'My boy Manuel together with David, Arturo, Bruno and Pedro attended last nights session at the old basketball court in Goleto with 17 other lads and they had a wonderful time,'

'Mr. Sam is very high on discipline and the lads like working with him, I really think it would be a wonderful idea to keep our young ones safe and off the streets,' She sat down embarrassed by the round of applause that greeted her little speech.

'Ok that's a yes then, I'll set it up with Mr. Lassiter.' said Sharon Clark.

While the teacher's sat down with the parents to discus there children's progress, Sharon Clark was flagged down by Sam.

'Hi Ms. Clark remember me I'm Sam Lassiter nice to meet you again,'

'Lets go to my office and see what you have got Mr. Lassiter,' Sam sat down in Ms. Clark's cramped office and opened his file with all the training sessions neatly presented. After he finished his run through he said 'That he had confirmation that his friend the Director of Marketing for Dolphin Sports and Leisure Ware will supply shirts, shorts and socks to Goleta Juniors in the specified School colours. As the sessions progress I have another sponsor who will supply the football boots. Finally my name is Sam to everybody on the Campus except the lads who seem to want to call me Coach.'

'That's wonderful Sam, can you start at the top field next Tuesday,' Next Tuesday it is Ms. Clark.' said Sam.

CHAPTER 12

Friday was just routine at the Clinic, although Sam spent a little time with a breast enhancement patient who was worried about the amount of bruising. 'Come and see me on Monday next and your troubles will be over.' said Sam.

Sam worked on his soccer training programme for next Tuesday and Thursday. He took a shower and changed into a polo shirt and khaki shorts and made his way over to Filippo's for his lunch date with David, Samantha and Monique. Sam was hoping to close a sponsorship deal with all three.

Both David and Monique agreed the deal which was wonderful for Sam and the boys, but in turn ok for the sponsor's to be known as supporters of the less fortunate. David said 'The shirts, shorts and socks would be sent to Sam before Saturday week,' and Monique said that she would attend the training session and get the required boot sizes from the lads.

Sam arrived early for the Thursday training session and set out 2 rows of road cones on the now beautiful mowed pitch. Thirty three lads turned up for the session and Sam put them to work immediately. As the lads did there 2 warm up laps he got them together. 'Welcome to you new guys, just a few rules to lay on you,' said Sam.

Any racist remarks are out, any that I hear means you are off the programme, are we clear on this,' A resounding "Yo" came from the assembled group. 'Now gather round in circles, do you remember the war cry,' "Dumas" yelled one of the Mexican kids. 'And why is that,' said Sam.

Becausse he wrote the Three Musketeers and we are using there motto "All for one and one for all", they all yelled.

'Ok lets here it,' said Sam.

"Dumas" they roared.

Sam spotted Principal Clark and a fit looking young women standing along side her. They were both watching the training session intensely, the lads dribbling in and out of the cones, some playing two touch, control and pass, while Sam was instructing two basketball players the art of Goalkeeping.

Sam blew his whistle and divided the lads into two teams. 'Lets see what you have got, 10 minutes each way, and with another blast on his whistle the game began.

As Principal Clark and the fit young lady approached Sam he didn't realize they were standing so close as he was concentrating on the match taking note of the lads showing a bit of quality.

Sam blew his whistle and said 'That's it guys until next Tuesday, work as hard in class as you do out here with me.'

'Good afternoon Mr. Lassiter, very impressive.'

'We're getting there Ma'am', said Sam as he collected up all the cones, corner flags. footballs and placed them into his borrowed van.

'I'd like to introduce you to Donna Douglas she's the Sports Coach here at Goleta Junior High,'

'Hi Donna, Sam Lassiter nice to meet you,'

As they were about to engage in conversation a bit of a skirmish was going on as the lads were leaving the field. Sam excused himself and sprinted to the bunch of boys who were facing up to each other.

'What's going on here,' said Sam.

'It's not fair Ramon has called my brother a retard and he's not, it's just that his legs don't work properly,' said Arturo. Sam had already noticed the little fella watching the training session from the sidelines his legs were in a mess as he zig zagged up and down following every kick.'

'Ramon did you say that,' 'Yes Coach' he said head bowed.

'Ok an apology now or you can take a walk,' said Sam.

'I'm sorry Coco,' said Ramon and they high fived.

'Coco will be my right hand man, he will carryout the following duties, water boy, oranges duties at half time and the supply of towels, is that ok with you Coco,'said Sam.

Coco's face beamed as he said 'Thanks Coach.'

As Sam was getting into his van Donna Douglas caught up with him. 'Sam after your presentation a lot of the parent's came up to me and said, what about the girls. I have no problems with that except that I know nothing about soccer,' said Donna.

'Every Tuesday and Thursday you are more than welcome to the training sessions and you can pick up a few training techniques,' said Sam.

'That would be great Sam,' said Donna.

The next three training sessions flew by and on the Thursday prior to the hand out of the kits, Sam got all the lads together. 'I would like you all to come here on Saturday at 2pm and bring your parent's if they can make it, you will be receiving shirts, shorts and socks free of charge and I wan't you to look after them, he continued. A lady will be present making a list of your shoe sizes, so be ready with that information, see you Saturday.'said Sam.

The Saturday arrived and Sam drove Filippo's van to the playing field, what greeted him was a beautifully prepared stretch of mown grass that could be compared with Wembley Stadium in the UK. Sam thought he must thank Manuel for this.

He off loaded a tent which would be used for the lads to change into there new gear, set up 4 collapsable tables. He was busy setting out the tent when Donna Douglas showed up with her Father.

'Just in time Donna, give us a hand with the tent please.' Within 10 minutes the tent was up and all guide ropes secured. Sam moved the tables in position. Table 1 for Monique to acquire the lads shoe sizes, Tables 2 and 3 for David and Samantha from Dolphin Leisureware to hand out the shirts, shorts and socks and Table 4 for Coco to hand out drinks and towels.

Mother's, Father's, relations and friends turned up with the lads and soon the two from the Dolphin Company were really busy.

Thirtysix young lads turned up and received there kit, went into the changing tent and returned to the field looking fantastic. The two basketball player's were decked out in all green outfits together with goalkeeping gloves. Sam was coaching the two keepers while Donna was supervising ball control techniques using the 3 rows of cones that Sam had already positioned.

The rest of the day went as planned with Monique taking action photo's of the lads and publicity photo's for Dolphin Leisurewear.

After the training session was completed Sam formed 3 groups for the all hands in chant. 'One two three "Dumas" they all yelled. 'I'll see you guys Tuesday 4pm.'

'See you Coach.' said the lads on there way back to there parents.

'I've reserved a table at Frankie and Jonny's resturant on 4th and Francis Avenue, I'll see you all there.' said Principal Clark.

Principal Sharon Clark standing up thanked David and Monique for there wonderful gifts to the lads soccer team. 'I can't thank you enough for your support, as you probably know we are continually fighting the school board for more funds to do our work more efficiently.'

'It's a pleasure to help in some way' said both David and Monique.

Chapter 13

The soccer season progressed and Sam had selected the 1st team squad of 17 players. The kids were really talented and ready for joining the under 12 league the following September. The last training session was conducted at the end of July and Sam informed the lads that training would commence the 1st week in September. He wished all the kids a happy summer holiday and told them to be careful.

Donna told Sam that she would like to take over some training in July and August and try and improve her coaching skills.

'Great idea Donna,' said Sam.

Sam returned to his boat settled down and then phoned Doctor Jon. 'I need time out from surgery Jon I'm going to devote my time to teaching kids some of the finer points of soccer at Goleta Junior High. I've been offered a full time coaching job and I want to give it my best shot,' said Sam.

'Not a problem Sam but don't be a stranger to me and my sister,' 'No chance of that Jon.' said Sam replacing the phone in it's holder.

Sam was working on a training programme for the next term starting in September when his phone rang.

'Hi Sam Lassiter,'

'Hello Sam it's Sharon Clark I've got some awful news for you, young Coco Martinez has been shot, he got caught in the crossfire between Black and Mexican drug pushers. He was out shopping for his Mom at an all night store when he was struck down, he is at present in intensive care at Santa Barbara General,'

'I'm on my way to the Hospital now,' said Sharon.

'I'll see you there.' said Sam.

The waiting area was silent apart from the gentle sob from Mrs. Martinez as Sam and Sharon sat down either side of her and offered as much comfort as they could. After a wait for over 3 hours the Surgeon finally appeared gown flecked with blood and looking ashen faced.

'I'm sorry Mrs. Martinez Coco didn't make it, he passed 10 minutes ago, the whole team worked frantically to save him but we didn't manage it, he lost to much blood, I'm so sorry.'

After ensuring that Mrs Martinez and Arturo had transport back to Goleta Sam sat in his car, he hadn't felt so bad since Janet's accident.

He arrived back at the boat and made a phone call to the Pentagon. 'High General,' said Sam. 'High yourself how are you,' said the General.

'I need a favour sir, two weeks today I need one of your Agents to pose for me and travel to New York, he can stay at the Penthouse on 5th Avenue. I need him to cover for me for 2 weeks while I sort out some minor players trying to be drug kings,'

'Not a problem 2 weeks today my man will be on his way to New York under your name.'

'Thank you sir.' said Sam.

Sam had already cleared it with Dr. Jon for the man to stay for a week at the Penthouse on 5th. He didn't even question why this was required, he new it must be important for Sam.

The church for Coco's funeral, Saint Mary's was packed to the rafters, with most of the congregation dressed conservatively wearing something black. The exception was the soccer team, Sharon Clark and Sam who wore the yellow with purple trim Goleta Junior High soccer shirts. Sam and Sharon sat either side of Mrs. Martinez and her son Arturo in the front row as requested by Mrs. Martinez.

During the service Sam gave a eulogy and just about managed it although the last part of his offering was delivered in no more than a whisper. He concluded by saying that Coco was well loved by all the soccer Mums and Dads and all playing members, he was my right hand man and I shall really miss him scooting up and down on match days giving his full attention to the players needs. God bless you Coco Martinez. He concluded by confirming that the number 31 shirt worn by Coco would be retired.

The funeral party dispersed and made there way to the Assembly Hall at Goleta Junior High where Sharon had laid on drinks and sandwiches. After an hour Mrs. Martinez gave Sharon and Sam a fairwell hug and left for her home with a tearful Arturo.

The Assembly room was now very quiet only the kitchen staff clearing all the dishes and removing all the chairs and tables. Sam sat alone in the corner thinking of the young life that had been so cruelly taken. Sharon quietly slipped on to the bench along side Sam and they both stared at each other neither of them uttering a word.

'We had better go,' said Sharon,

'Yes you are right,'said Sam as they both stood up. Sharon then put both arms around Sam's neck and they stayed locked together to what seemed a lifetime. Sam kissed her on the cheek, said goodby and left the building.

The following day Sam made a call to one of the Charity Shops in Santa Barbara, he purchased a some well worn shirts, jumpers, trousers, an overcoat and a pair of ladies ear warmers. He then went on to the wig shop and purchased a long grey wig. His final visit was to the local tip where he picked up a disgarded Supermarket trolley. He placed all his purchases in the back of Filippo's pick up truck that he had borrowed and returned to the "Jon Jo".

Sam's research and surveillance was meticulous and after two nights was ready to go. It was midnight on the 4th as Sam set off pushing his trolley the 3 miles to the area he had targeted. The local bag ladies and rough sleeping guys were located on the west side of the Santa Barbara Freeway just secluded under one of the many flyovers. One Hundred yards away from a Burger van where the black druggies and pushers hang out till the early hours. Sam approached the rough sleepers camp and was met by a huge bear like guy.

'What the hell do you want,' he said,

'I want to crash out with you guys I'm really shot', said Sam.

'We have room here but I'm not sure whether we want you, we have only a limited supply of cannabis and hard liquor and not enough to include you,' said the bear like bloke.

'I don't do shit and I don't drink but I have a buying in present for you guys,' said Sam pulling out a bottle of scotch and handing it to the big fella.

'That will do nicely, welcome, what's your name,'

'Many thanks,' as he sorted out his sleeping area using his old sleeping bag, a blanket and some rejected carboard boxes.

'The names Sammy', he said.

When the six other guys and the old biddy were asleep Sam eased his way out of his bag and quietly moved towards the Burger van which was now closed. He placed a pick up microphone in two places one under the front side of the van and the other hidden in a dark corner adjacent to where the black guys regularly assembled. He then placed an explosive device radio activated under the Burger van with enough C4 to cause a large bang.

The next day Sam sat around a fire devil with the rest of the lads as Cleo busied herself sorting out her pram for the 20th time. They all went to bed at around 9pm. Sam switched on the receiving electrics and plugged in his ear phones which he covered with the pink ladies ear muffs. He drew a blank that night and for the next two nights, then on night three he struck gold.

The top man a Clyde Thompson was holding court with 5 other pushers. They collected in a close formation ready for Clyde's orders. 'We have a delivery this morning at 3am, you Rick and you Danny will be with me to collect, come tooled up in case our Mexican friends try to take us down, if it's anything like the last time it will be just shooting practice for us.' Danny spoke up 'Yeh we nailed 5 of those fuckin wet backs and put a couple of slugs into some retard.' he said.

'Got you, you bastards', Sam whispered to himself.

He waited until all the guys were standing ready to be served in front of the van. He hit the switch and the explosion was loud and devastating with all the body parts spread over an area 30 feet. The burger stand was no more, just a crumpled mess.

Sam left the area and made his way through the dark streets of Goleta back to his boat where he showered shaved and got rid of all the tatty clothes in the Marina dump skip.

The following morning he tuned in to the local TV news station who confirmed that they think 6 bodies had been found, this was proving difficult due to the devastating effect of the explosion. On the face of it the Police believe it was a tit for tat for the deaths of the 5 Mexicans during a recent clash. The Police are trying to trace the person who manufactured the explosive device as it was professionally designed.

Sam phoned the General in Virginia to confirm that the substitute Sam Lassiter had returned to LA from New York.

Sam sat in the lounge of the Jon Jo and wrote to Trisha, Katherine and Len Jackson and informed them that he would try and get over to the UK for Christmas. In the quietness of his surroundings Sam put an idea in motion so that Coco's name would not be forgotten and he ran his idea across Principal Clark.

She gave his idea a blessing and Sam immediately phoned Donna with his plans. He listed the best 8 players at Goleta Junior High and asked Donna to select 5 other players to go along side the 8 quality players. A six a side competition would take place Saturday week for the Martinez Trophy. Sam would arrange a trophy, 6 imitation gold medals, 6 silver and 36 bronze, to be presented by Mrs. Martinez if she is up to it and the famous actress Desiree de Carlo.

CHAPTER 14

Sam was just about to wander across to the US Postal with his letters when the phone rang.

'Hi Sam good morning, Sergeant Carpenter would like to report for duty,'

'What did you have in mind Des,' said Sam

'A nice few days away from the hustle and bustle of show business would be great,' said Des,'

'Come on over it would be like old times, come to the Santa Barbara Marina and ask the guy on the gate to direct you to the "Jon Jo".

Three hours later Desiree de Carlo arrived at Sam's boat, she was greeted with a huge hug from Sam. 'That's the closest you have ever got to me Sam you were always the perfect gentleman,' Sam showed Des to her cabin and let her settle in, 'I'll see you on the upper sun deck, wear as least as possible as we can get in some sun time,' said Sam.

Sam was lying on the sun bed when Des entered the sun deck.

'You look beautiful', said Sam viewing the very brief white bikini.

Desiree was 5 feet 10 inches tall with not an inch of fat, with a body to die for, her long dark waist length hair beautively coffuired. She laid down along side Sam and interlocked hands.

'Remind you of anything,' said Des.

'Korea 1952 – 53, but the view is better staring at the deep blue California sky.'

'Beats the mosquito net doesn't it,' said Des.

As they laid there soaking up the rays Des removed her hand and placed it gently on Sam's already hard penis.

'In over a year we lived and slept in the same tent and not once did you hit on me, all the other MASH personnel thought that we were an item,'

'A few things really,' said Sam,

'I was quite happy with everyone thinking that we were a couple, in fact it gave me a bit of a buzz that I was linked to the best looking girl in the whole of Korea,'

'The main reason for not coming on to you was the fact that I'm probably the worlds worst lover and I didn't want to look and feel an idiot,' said Sam.

'I could have nursed you through that Sam, you were and still are a very attractive man,' slipping easily out of her bikini and removing Sam's swim pants.

'Lay back and think of England Sam I've been waiting to do this for 3 years,' said Des.

She straddled Sam and gently eased herself down on his erect manhood, she soon realised a slow sensual rythym sighing quietly on every downward movement. The tempo of there lovemaking suited Sam. After a while Desi increased the tempo and was working her way towards a huge orgasm.

'I think it's time whispered Sam,' as they both climaxed together.

Desi collapsed on top of Sam motionless and they stayed in this position for an age without uncoupling. 'That was worth waiting 3 years for,' said Desi.

Desi agreed to help Mrs. Martinez present the prizes at the six a side tournament on the following Saturday. 'Your fans, Parents and kids will love you to bits Des,' said Sam.

The six a side competion was a great success and Arturo's side one the gold with Ramon's team picking up the silver. All the other players received a bronze medal. The cup was presented to Arturo by Mrs. Martinez and Desiree de Carlo. One hundred and thirty people attended the meet and had a wonderful time. Sharon Clark had a permanent smile on her face as she walked the crowd with Miss de Carlo.

Sharon caught up with Sam and thanked him for a wonderful day and added that she is looking forward to him being part of the teaching team for the next term.

CHAPTER 15

Sam spent the Sunday relaxing and preparing for the Christmas term by fine tuning his training programme. He also completed a series of sessions for Donna Douglas.

He had a chat with Jon and Monique and got a letter off to Katherine in the UK. Sam was having a little doze when the phone broke the peaceful silence. 'High Sam, General Richards how are you stranger,' 'I'm good' said Sam how have you been keeping sir,' said Sam.

'Pretty good form really Sam, I want you to have a look at something for me down at San Diego Naval Base, it's to. complicated to discuss on the phone I'll mail it to you if you except the mission,'

'Mail it sir of course I'll except it,' said Sam.

The next day special delivery mail arrived from the Pentagon and Sam went through it detail. Apparently some US Navy women Officers from San Diego Naval Base had been taken and fed the truth drug and parting with secret information. The information relating to the patrols of the Nuclear submarines is like gold dust to perspective enemies of the US, together with US troop movements around the world.

The Intelligence Section here is located 10 miles north of San Diego bay near the Marine Base at Camp

Pendleton. The US Navy didn't like interferance from outside sources they preferred to handle the situation internally without any input by the FBI or the CIA.

General Clint Matthews US Marines was the man who Sam was to report to. Matthews was a huge man well over six four with a huge barrel chest.

'Good to meet you Colonel, General Richards has filled me in on your background, it seems you made a few of those Japanese bastards jump around a bit.'

'Jungle warfare suited me and my men sir they took to it like ducks to water,' said Sam.

'We will get these bastards I'm not sure they are the brightest in the world, they are going to make a mistake soon and then we will nail them.' Sam continued. 'They are using old hat methods to get information from our girls using the so called truth drug, it's a serum with Amobarbital as one of it's components it makes you feel you have had one to many beers. It's old hat sir, used by the Nazi's in WW2.

'We need to nail these assholes sooner rather than later, or they will be telling us where our Nuclear subs are,' said General Matthews.

'I normally work alone sir, I'll give you an update within a week,'said Sam.

'If you do need any assistance you know where my office is Colonel,'

'What are your initial requirements Colonel,' said Matthews.

'I need an appartment overlooking the entrance to building 29 which I believe houses the more senior secret service personnel, I also need 2 pairs of powerful binoculars one fixed on the occupants board and one on a stand purely for observation, I need a camera with a photo electric zoom and a truck full of coffee,' said Sam.

'All will be made available for you within an hour,'

'Ok I need to get busy with the old fashioned Police work i.e. Stakeouts,' said Sam.

Sam pulled the mattress off the bed in his temporary o accomodation and placed it on the floor a step back from the window in the darker area of the room, he set up the binoculars and the camera and was ready for the long haul of surveillance.

Sam made contact with General Matthews and asked for 2 surveillance teams to be located just outside the Naval Apartments, one in a burger restaurants's car park facing south towards downtown San Diego and one parked in a gas station facing north.

After more than 48 hours of nothing of significant interest Sam noticed not for the first time a lovely looking all American California beach babe riding into the car park on a scooter which had painted on the rear carrier box "Charlie's Pizza's". She was following closely a Navy registered vehicle. A tall smartly dressed woman in her summer uniform stepped out of the vehicle and made her way to the entrance of the building. The scooter driver peeled off her pink crash helmet and closely followed the Navy Captain to the building entrance.

'Hi i'm looking for Miss Slater but she doesn't seem to be on the indicator, damb nuisance this has happened before,' said the blonde pizza girl. As she turned away from the door she noticed and made a note of the Navy Captains apartment number.

She returned to her scooter and took out a pen and wrote something on the pizza box. Started the engine as was off.

Sam radioed the two surveillance vehicles, 'Standby gentlemen we may have something, a busty blonde with tiny pink shorts riding a pizza scooter is on her way towards you I think she will be going towards downtown, find out her destination guys and take some photographs. One more thing don't let her see you,' said Sam.

'We're on it Colonel.'

Sam fished out his street map of downtown San Diego and set off in pursuit of his surveillance teams. 'You are right Colonel she's headed south towards the city. She stopped and parked up outside an apartment block and sounded the bell and after a few moments a young foreign looking teenager appeared and took the pizza package, he excused himself for a moment and then returned with a couple of little see through bags with what looked like happy powder. The delay in the man going of to get the drugs gave the surveillance teams time to fire off some photo's. The teenager dwelt for a moment at the door o his apartment eye balling the pizza girls tight ass. This slight pause gave Sam's men a chance to get some more pictures.

Sam arrived about 10 minutes after the surveillance teams and joined them in there vehicles. 'I think I got the flat number I can get it blown up and get some names,' said Captain Evans one of the surveillance crew lads.

'Ok lets find out who these people are and we'll go from there, who owns this building anyway,' said Sam.

'I'm on it,' said Evans.

The owners were contacted and 6 men lived at number 36, 2 at College, 2 at Freeway Tyres and 2 working at Pier 43 as Forklift truck drivers.

'Stay here and keep an eye on the building, I need to know every movement they make, I've got a feeling about these guys,' said Sam as he left the area and returned to watch over the Navy Captains apartment.

Sam phoned General Matthews and asked for a warrant to enter and search apartment 43 at Bayswater Park.

Sam got on the Radio to Jordan and Evans, and asked was there any movement.

'Quiet as a mouse,' said Evans.

'Wait a minute we have movement both parties on there way out probably to screw around with Captain Parkinson,'

'When they have left get into the apartment and have a good look around and take photographs,' said Sam.

Sam then phoned General Matthews 'sir get your men to Pier 43 and pick up 2 Forklift driver's Gregory and Marple aka Schroder and Elster.'

As Sam waited for the 2 men who were to pay a visit to Captain Stella Parkinson the phone rang and it was Jordan.

They have Nazi memrobelia all over the apartment pictures of Adolf and of the Hitler Youth parades. Bomb making plans and enough E4 to take out the whole city. Exploded views of the Nuclear Sub were laid out on a table and a red cross marked the spot where the bomb was to be placed.'

'Ok wait for the two students to arrive back from College and arrest them and shove them in the slammer, General Matthews is bringing in the 2 guys from Pier 43,'

'I'll handle "Pinkie and Perky" at Parkinson's place.'

Sam asked the General to contact Captain Parkinson to allow him to enter her apartment. Sam entered Stella's place and let himself into her bedroom. He explained what he wanted her to do and told her not to worry as he would always be in control.

Twenty minutes later the door bell rang, 'Water Board, there is a leak in the building and it looks like it is in your apartment, can we come in please it won't take a minute,' he said raising his hand holding some kind of ID.

Stella opened the door and let the two men into her apartment, they quickly gagged her, sat her in a chair taping her hands and feet to a chair.

'When is the Nuclear sub the USS Nautilus docking in San Diego and at what pier number,'

'I am not privy to that information and if I was I wouldn't tell you,' she said.

The man smacked her across the face and jammed some truth drug concoction into her mouth. 'Now where were we,' said the young Nazi.

Sam burst through the bedroom door and shouted 'get your fuckin hands up you pair of creeps,' The leader turned towards Sam his Luger in his hand, he didn't get the chance to fire it as Sam shot him in the face killing him instantly.

'What about you you pussy, do you want some,'

'Please no I can't stand pain,' he said

'You can't stand pain yet you can watch your dead buddy here inflict it on young ladies, you make me sick,' said Sam.

Sam looked disgusted and as he turned fired a shot into the guys knee cap. The guy screamed and sang like a canary.

Sam completed his summary of the mission and presented to the General and Chiefs of Staff US Navy at San Diego. The whereabouts of key personnel was obtained using the pizza girls who were paid in the form of drugs, all six arrested are fanatical Neo Nazi's obsessed with the Fuhrer and with one thought in mind to give the USA a bombing they would always remember and maybe give a thought to the civilians killed in Berlin and Dresden in WW2. If they had managed to get a bomb on board one of our Nuclear Subs half of San Diego would disappear.'

'I would like to thank the Navy surveillance team for doing a great job and to praise Captain Parkinson for her bravery.'

I've got to leave now gentlemen I have a lot of young lads waiting for me in Santa Barbara for soccer practice.'

Sam eased the Ferarri up to 100 miles an hour on his way home.

CHAPTER 16

Sam eased the Ferarri into the Marina parking lot and killed the big V6 engine. He sat motionless for a brief moment listening to the chatter of rigging and all the familiar sounds of tethered boats. Filippo appeared at the rear of the building taking out a couple of bags of garbage and bursting into song along with his hero Mario Lanza.

'A lasagne to go please Filippo,' said Sam,

'Got it, get your bum in here and have a coffee,' said Filippo.

Sam collected his take a way lunch and settled down in the top lounge of the "Jon Jo", to review his timetable for next weeks training sessions. Sam looked up at the TV and saw landing craft hitting the beach and what looked like Royal Marines disembarking. He turned the volume up to catch what the reported had to say. 'At 4am this morning 40 Commando and 42 Commando hit the shore at Port Said, 45 Commando arriving in helecopters captured the adjacent air field with the 3rd Battalian Paratroopers and the French Foreign Legion beached on the west side of the Suez Canal at Port Fued.

Sam placed a call to General Farquason-Keith to find out more.

'Hello dear boy,' he boomed.

'What's going on Sir, I'm just watching the TV coverage,'

'Nasser has nationalised the bloody Suez Canal and the Israeli's, the French and the Brits don't like it. So Anthony Eden gave the order to attack. Within 48 hours the landing forces were in complete control of the city and waiting for the call to advance further towards Cairo.'

'Then a set back, the Americans didn't like the show of force and Eisenhower seeking re-election was adament on this. The value of the Sterling dropped dangerously low and Eisenhower refused to help unless the French and the Brits ceased hostilities.' Anthony Eden now a really sick man pulled the plug and the shock troops left the area and returned to there bases in Cyprus, Malta and North Africa. 'Nasser became a hero to the whole Arab world as the man who stood up to the imperial coilition of France and Great Brittain and had defeated them,' said the General. 'Don't worry Sam he'll get his sooner or later.'

'So that's it Sam, when are you coming over to the UK again, I think the time is right to get you and Jackson front and centre, I set something up'

'Ok General, see you soon, will advise on ETA London and pop in a see you.' Sam replaced the phone in it's holder.

CHAPTER 17

The soccer programme was settling in nicely and the kids loved it. Sam was gradually moulding the Goleta Junior High first eleven, ready for stepping into the Junior league. The side would start in the third division, the first match the 2nd Saturday in October.

A good crowd turned out for the first match, not only girls and boys but most parents of the players hugged the touchlines. Sam got the lads together and said 'I don't care if we get beaten 10 to zip as long as we play our passing game and not go running all over the field like scolded rabbits.

The Ref blew his whistle and the game began, it was a no contest as Goleta passed the opposition off the park, running out winners by 7 to nil. Sam gave the opponents coach a hand shake and was pleased to see that the team doing the same. One loud "Dumas" and all adjourned to the gym for drinks and snacks.

The Michaelmas Term at Goleta Junior High moved serenely into early December, with Sam feeling more at home and taking to the full time coaching job,

Principal Clark was delighted that Sam had settled in and thought that Sam had brought a breath of fresh air to the Staff Room. Even old Henry Briggs the thorny old history teacher seemed to come alive when Sam entered the room.

Donna Douglas was now officially coach of the 2nd and 3rd eleven sides, these were mostly 9 and 10 year olds who needed nursing and TLC, which she handed out in spades. The young ones loved her which in any coach is a good sign.

The first eleven Sam's pride and joy sat on top of Division 3 well clear of any of the other sides. Played 8, won 8, it doesn't get ant better than that. To watch 11 year old kids showing off there skills, control, tackling, positional sense, these kids had the lot.

Scouts from professional Mexican League sides were ever present watching the progress of certain *individuals.* The parents of Arturo, Henri and Alex had been approached and told the scouts that they would do nothing until Coach Lassiter gave his blessing.

Sam bumped into Donna outside the Staff Room, 'Hey Donna I've got some training seesion notes I need to run across you, can we meet after school somewhere,' said Sam.

'Yeh nice idea I'll see you in Lucy's next door to Anderson's Arcade in Santa Barbara,' said Donna.

Sam parked his Ferrari next to Donna's tiny Ford Pinto in Lucy's car park. He entered the dimly lighted bar with soft romantic music just loud enough so as not to restrict conversation. He spotted Donna sitting in a quiet corner on a bench seat, Sam slid in beside her, 'Ok lets get a beer and a snack,' said Sam.

They both ordered a Bud and a burger and french fries from a waitress with the tiniest mini skirt that Sam had ever seen. As she walked away Sam nodded his head and Donna seeing this burst into laughter.

Sam spread the new coaching schedules all across the table, he paused and had a look around the club and noted that all the pairs were same sex, laughing and enjoying each others company.

'Donna I think I'm in the wrong place babe,' said Sam.

'Your fine Sam my friend, ok this is a place for people who care for each other, many who have had a bad experience in so called normal relationships. I'm one of them, I'm not a lesbian but after a nasty breakup with a fella I have found someone who has really made me happy with myself again.'

'I completely understand that Donna and admire all the people here and you especially with all the crass remarks that you are not supposed to hear, but you do.

'You may have guessed that I have lesbian tendencies, although I try to laugh them off at school, so as not to make them to obvious,' she said.

'All I know is you are a beautiful girl and a bloody good Coach and if you have a lovely friend then that's wonderful too,' said Sam.

CHAPTER 18

The itinery for the European trip arrived a day later, it read:

Depart Northolt 0900 on December 7th, travel to St. Andrews barracks and deliver lecture to 40 Commando.

Deliver the same lecture to 45 Comando at Mtarfa on Wednesday the 9th

Depart Malta 10th to Northolt, ETA apprx. 1600 hours.

Complete the programme at Lympstone and finally the Commando School at Bickleigh, on 15th and 16th.

The whole trip was a huge success and the extra footage from Movietone News added additional interest.

'Those lads needed that said the General after the bashing they had from the press.'

The three of them travelled together from Bickleigh in the Generals staff car, dropping off Sam at Sunningdale and Len at King's Cross railway station. 'Lets do it again next year,' said the General.

CHAPTER 19

Christmas at the Manor was something else, a wonderful table with beautively prepared lunch and of course Lance's favourite tipple a really expensive chablis. It was a real family affair something that Sam had never experienced. Lance and his lovely wife and two little daughters and Katherine and her latest beau and the still gorgeous Trisha and little Thomas.

After lunch the children played in the paddock with Katherine in charge as she let all the children ride on Soloman the handsome hunter. While all the adults watched the children having a wonderful time Sam quietly wandered down to Janet's art gallery. A few new paintings had been purchased since Sam's last visit. He sat down on a bench seat opposite a Degas his mind racing back to the romantic time he spent with Janet in New York. Sam was hurting badly as he dropped his head in his hands when Trisha slid in beside him on the bench seat.

'I bet it hurts like hell,' she said

'Just a bit Trish,' said Sam

Trisha wrapped her arms around Sam and held him really tight. Sam stayed perfectly still throughout the embrace not moving an inch just remembering how much he truly loved Janet.

'I have loved a few times in my life Trisha, but circumstances prevented me from making it a permanent option, the business I was in didn't lend itself to any kind of lasting relationship.

'My job working with the Pentagon is a potentially dangerous one and to commit to one person wouldn't be fair as any moment I could be dead,' said Sam,

'When we were together I thought that was the case especially as I had already lost someone,' said Trisha,

'I'd basically retired from active service when Janet and I got together and as the pressure was lifted somewhat I could hopefully concentrate on less violent future. Then the bloody accident which near as dammit killed me.'

'I know it's hard Sam but try to think of the wonderful time although short that you had together,' said Trisha,

'I don't know how you do it Trisha, not once but twice you have lost someone very dear, I just don't know how the hell you do it,' said Sam,

'We must have done something really bad to upset the governor in heaven for him to take our three loved ones away from us,'

'You are not only beautiful, you are a wonderful mother to Thomas and someone I will always treasure.' said Sam. They both sat quietly on the bench clinging to each other in Janet's gallery.

The rest of the day was more relaxing with Sam taking over the playing with the children duties while Lance, Katherine and Trisha took time out. After dinner all the kids jumped into the showers and were whisked off to bed. Sam retired to his room, packed ready for an early off in the morning. Lance had arranged for Spencer to drive Sam to the new London Airport at Heathrow in the morning. On the way to the Airport Spencer asked 'How's the MG Sam,'

'Sold her to a collector in California and got a great deal on a Ferrari Spyder,' said Sam

'I bet that flies,' said Spencer

'Like a bird.' said Sam.

Sam slept soundly more or less all the way to New York, only the clunk of the undercarriage being set down woke him up. He cleared customs and immigration and made his way to New York Airways and took the chopper to La Guardia. Sam boarded the plane and it set off for LA.

CHAPTER 20

Sam settled down in the flying bridge of the "Jon Jo" and waded through his mail that had backed up during his absence in the UK. He put aside the letters from the UK and concentrated on the ones with the Virginia postmark. The letter from the General was a long drawn out affair and needed Sam's full attention. It read:

As you are more than aware we in the United States of America have a Constitution, in which there are many amendments, the most frequently used is the 5th, normally by our friends the Italian Mafioso. The first amendment is a guarantee of freedom of speech, which allows political and minority organisations to demonstrate and vent there feelings. Stepping close to going outside the perameters of late is the Neo-Nazi Party, encouraging racist and anti semetic activities. The word on the street is that the Nazi's are planning a protest march straight through the middle of a highly populated jewish community in Chicago.

The Neo Nazi's started making noises in 1958, having originally been the United States Right Party, run by two guys, an Edward Fields and J.B.Jones. The party are very active with a high profile and causing problems for the local Chicago PD and the FBI. The national and local press, TV and radio are giving the law enforcement people a bad press accusing them of excessive force and of course the Nazi's are milking this. So Sam I want you to get in on the ground floor here and do what you normally do, that is cause chaos. So it's also an ass covering exercise for the boys in blue. Sam opened the other large envelope from Virginia and studied all the main players in the Chicago Neo-Nazi Party. Finally the air ticket was attached along with his hotel reservation in the Northside of Chicago. Before departing Sam phoned Sharon Clark and informed her that he will be absent from school for maybe a week, away on government business.

'Ok Sam we have been expecting this haven't we, ill see you soon as, I'll let Donna off the leash,' she said.

'She can handle it.' said Sam.

Sam travelled to Chicago the next morning

By tea time he was nicely ensconced in the Mayflower hotel in the North side of the windy city. He telephoned Chicago PD and asked to speak with Detective Gerry Patterson.

'One moment please, who's calling,' said the operator.

'Sam Lassiter from Santa Barbara, the call is expected,'

'Good afternoon Sam Lassiter my name is Geraldine Patterson, did you have a good trip?,'

There was a slight pause as Sam answered.

'Sorry I thought Gerry was a guy, sorry if I sounded a tad surprised,' said Sam,

'That's ok Mr. Lassiter it's not the first time,' she said.

'By the way the names Sam, lets get together and run this thing through Gerry,' said Sam.

'I'll be there at the Mayflower in twenty minutes,' said Gerry.

Sam waited in the reception area for Detective Patterson. A tall elegant lady dressed predominately in black entered the hotel, her dark hair bobbing from side to side as she strode like a model towards him. Sam ushered her to a window table and they sat down opposite each other.

'Nice to meet you Gerry,'

'Back to you Sam,'

Sam studied the detail especially the layout of the building that housed the workshop of the Neo-Nazi Party.

'A package arrived for you Sam from Virginia special delivery,' Sam viewed the package and smiled as he opened the package.

'It's a tranquilliser gun Gerry with a couple of spare darts, we will have to put Adolf the guy on the front desk to sleep for three hours,' said Sam.

It was a six story office block just off Dearborn in the northern side of the windy city.

'We managed to get an undercover police women on the cleaning staff in here and she was able to give an accurate layout,' Sam studied the floor layout, top floor just s storage area and of no interest, the fifth floor housed two printing machines, the forth three giant photo copying machines, the third a sorting room, the second floor was the memorabilia room with brown shirts, black ties and swastika arm bands. The first floor was the reception area with someone stationed at the front desk 24/7. Finally the lower ground floor where three vehicles equipped with radio transmitters were parked.

'We are going in from the roof, a helicopter drop would be ok, the noise level would only be aparent for less than a minute,' said Sam.

'I can go even better, we have a new Bell helicopter Model 47 and they have developed a less noisy system fitted to the engine and rotor blades, it's not completely silent, more of a whispering sound, the good people of Chicago didn't like there sleep interupted by excessive noise levels after midnight,' said Gerry.

'Thank you Chicago,' said Sam. Sam gave Gerry a list of requirements for our monday night soiuree:

Black face masks
Black all in one suits
Black SV boots
Weapons with back up magazines
Hand pump and black dye
Bolt croppers
Tranquillizer gun

'We will rehearse tomorrow get a good days rest on Monday and will meet up at the Helipad on Tuesday at 0100 hours.

Tuesday 0100 hours Sam and Gerry were strapped into the Bell helicopter and were weaving there way through the skyscrapers of Chicago towards the target area, the pilot shifted the controls into quiet mode as he closed in on the target rooftop. He hovered 4 feet from the roof as both passengers jumped from the helicopter, followed later by Sam's back pack. The helicopter moved silently away en-route back to the police headquarters.

Sam used the bolt croppers to remove the lock which it did with ease and carefully opened the roof top door. He directed the beam of his torch all around the opening and no trip wires or alarms were present. They both slipped through the door and quickly decended to floor 5. He left Gerry on the 4th floor, held up one finger to his lips and followed it up with a hand raised five finger gesture that he would return in five minutes. Sam used the stairs down to the reception area and there was Adolf head bowed half asleep at his desk. The man's position was perfect to receive the dart, a big fat hairless neck waiting to be plugged. Sam moved to within four feet and fired the dart into the man's neck, within three seconds the man was out for the count. Sam returned to the 4th floor and told Gerry to get busy, she quickly produced two black fullscap papers and a larger one and placed them into the three photo copying machines, she fed in propaganda material into the feeder and started printing, checking that the complete text was obliterated and all that was left was a view of Chicago by night.

Sam went up to floor five and set about destroying the printing press, he released nuts and bolts and completely smashed the drive mechanism, all the parts he ruined he sent down the garbage shoot, this would be picked up at 6am. He then went down to the lower ground level via the reception area to collect the keys for the vehicles and to check on Adolf. The man was stirring and making strange noises so Sam gave him another shot with the stun gun. Sam popped the bonnets of the three vehicles and removed the distributor and the leads, severed all hydraulic and water hoses and removed the carburettor's from all three vehicles. He then smashed the sump and let the oil flow all over the tarmac. His final act was to smash the radio transmitters to bits. He returned to Gerry who was nearing the end of her printing exercise, he moved in on Floor 2 the memorabelia room set up his hand pump and sprayed the whole room black, completely rubbishing brown shirts, swastika's and anything that looked Neo-Nazi. Gerry and Sam re-pact the now defunked propaganda leaflets and transferred them to floor 3. They collected all there gear and let themselves out through the main door locking it behind them and throwing the key into the nearest drain. Before he left the building Sam left two envelopes, inside the first was a note: I am not a member of any law enforcement body, not Police, FBI, CIA, I'm just a guy who has a problem with evil people and you Nazi's are evil people. If I get to hear of any Jewish, black or gypsy being violated, killed or injured then I will return and there will be violence, you have been warned. The second message envelope contained a verse that Sam suggested they sing when on one of there propaganda marches. It read:

> Hitler has only got one ball
> Goring has two but rather small
> Himmler has something simler
> But poor old Gobals has no balls at all.

They ran 200 yards to the pre arranged pick up point and were whisked away back to Chicago Police Headquarters.

Gerry drove Sam to O'Hare airport later that day and said in parting,

'Thanks for putting a word in for me with the Captain Sam,'

'Hey it was a pleasure to be working with a pro, if these idiots get a bit frisky in the future maybe we can get together again I'm a tad better with the violent stuff than I am as an equipment basher,' said Sam.

She dropped Sam off at the departures and gave him a little kiss.

'I've left my card in your desk, if you ever want to come down to Santa Barbara away from the windy city you are welcome, there's plenty of room on the boat.' said Sam.

CHAPTER 21

Sam's flight was delayed 1 hour so he telephoned Principal Clark and informed her that he would be back on the payroll before the 4pm soccer session. Finally a weary Sam boarded the plane to LA, slumped into his seat and slept the whole trip. He arrived early evening in Los Angeles and took the Greyhound to Santa Barbara, then decided to walk the two miles to the marina.

The following morning Sam parked the Ferrari in his reserved spot and was just getting out of his vehicle when Donna's Ford Pinto roared past him, he could see that she was stressed, red eyes and tears streaming. Principal Clark emerged from the building waving for Donna to slow down, this was all in vain as Donna's tyres screeched on the tarmac.

'Damn men,' said Sharon Clark,

'What's the problem Sharon,' said Sam,

'That idiot Chester Clemence has just called her a "Dyke" in front of all the teaching staff,'

Sam didn't have much to do with Clemence he came across as a know all asshole and full of it, but maybe in the near future Sam would be paying him a visit.

'I have suspended Mr. Clemence until further notice, I shall be interviewing the whole staff individually to hear what they have to say,' said the worried Principal.

'Can you sit in for Clemence for me Sam, it's mainly a geography review with 3A.'

Sam did two periods with 3A and enjoyed it, they were concentrating on the far east which was right up Sam's alley. He took two soccer sessions in the afternoon one his and the other Donna's.

Sam finished the soccer training and went along to the staff room to find it crowded out with the teaching staff.

'I don't care what you say, Donna was not a lesbian,' said Miss Walters the biology teacher.

'She is just a lovely girl and we want her back,' said Tom Varley the history teacher.

'Just because she lives with another woman doesn't mean she is a lesbian, for goodness sake I've lived with a number of guys in my life but I'm not a homosexual,' said Sam

'Just one more thing while I'm on my soapbox, it wouldn't bother me one iota if she was a lesbian or if any member of our staff was a homosexual as long as they leave it at home and don't shout about it, if they are nice people and good at there job then that's fine with me.' said Sam.

Principal Clark then said that 'Donna wasn't answering her phone and she had no idea where she was,'

''I think I know where she is,' said Sam.

'Great I'll come with you,'

'I think not Sharon if the paparazzi get a shot of you going into "Lucy's" bar, it would be all over the front page of every paper in California, it's a girl girl and a boy boy bar, where they can go and relax and feel safe away from morons like Clemence.'

Sam drove straight to Lucy's and parked the Ferarri next to Donna's little Ford, he entered the bar and soon located Donna sat in a corner booth.

'Hi coach,' said Sam,

'Hi yourself,' said a tearful Donna.

'Clemence has been suspended and will most probably loose his job, which is great news, all the teaching staff and I mean all, want you to come back to work, you are a much loved member of the team and bloody good at what you do,' said Sam,

'It's been a bad couple of days Sam, Beth has left the apartment and has a new job in Miami and then of course the Clemence business. I'm going to have to leave the apartment as it's to expensive for just one person I really can't be bothered to chase a new flatmate,' said Donna,

'I have an idea, why don't you come and live on my boat, you've seen it and there is plenty of room, you could loose yourself in the damn thing and the rent would be free,' said Sam.

'What do I have to do to if I say yes,'

'You have to come back to work tomorrow and keep yourself fed, the rent is free and you can stay for as long as you like until you find a place of your own again,'

'Deal,' said Donna.

'Pay your bills and start to move in at the week-end,' said Sam giving her a huge bear hug.

'See you tomorrow at school,' said Donna.

They both left Lucy's at the same time and drove off in different directions. When Sam reached the comfort of his upper lounge he placed a call to the General in Virginia.

Can you check out someone for me sir, his name is Chester Clemence he is a teacher at Goleta Junior High. He originates from the Tampa area in Florida, can you see if he is clean sir,' said Sam.

'I'm on it,' the General said.

'Excellent job in Chicago Sam, the Nazi's are in a hell of a mess, nice uncomplicated mission, picture perfect,'

'The girl Detective Geraldine Patterson of Chicago PD is one you should be monitoring sir, she's good,' said Sam.

'Duly noted Sam, I'll be in touch.' said the General slipping his phone in the cradle.

The next day was back to normal at Goleta Junior High, Donna was greeted with hugs all round even from the shy Tom Varley the history teacher. Sam took over the geography lessons that were vacated by Clemence, fortunately the era was 1940–42 and the impact of WW2 on London and the British nation. Sharon had already requested for a temporary teacher. Sam passed Sharon in the main walkway and she pointed in the direction of her office and suggested that he join her.

'I think Clemence is going for wrongful dismissal, I don't want that man anywhere near my students,' she said.

'I can understand that Sharon but it's very difficult to get rid of poor quality teachers, there contracts now are more or less fireproof,' said Sam.

'I have called on a friend to get the drop on our Mr. Clemence, if he has been a bad boy then my man will find it,'

'Appreciate that Sam.'

Sam arrived at the boat early evening to find a large envelope on the upper deck floor, post marked Virginia.

Hello Sam, Mr. Oliver Chester Harrington was prosecuted on 21st January 1947 in a Tampa Bay court for fondling small girls and boys, he was fired from his teaching job and given two years suspended sentence in an institution. After two years he was released, changed his name to Chester Clemence. By fair means or foul he altered all his teacher training certificates to read Chester Clemence. While he was in the institution his wife left him and also obtained an order preventing him from making contact with his two children. He managed to bluff his wat into Gorleta Junior High in 1950. Suggest that the school board at Goleta tighten up on pre interview information. My last comment would be that if he's done it once he'll do it again.

Sam immediately phoned Principal Clark.

'Got the bastard,' said Sam and went all the way through the correspondence with Sharon.

'Thank you so much Sam, we've got him he dare not take us to court now.'

The rest of the term went by without any problems it was nice to see Donna back in the swing of things loving her job and living quarters on the Jon Jo, she had also not paid one visit to Lucy's since that fateful day.

The summer holidays came along and Sam was determined to have a good rest, he had decided not to go over to the UK this summer, instead he would take an extra week at Christmas.

The close knit Teacher's Union would make it difficult for Clemence to find a teaching post especially in Southern California.

CHAPTER 22

Sam was getting used to Donna moving around the boat with next to nothing on, that, thought Sam was a site worth looking at. She seemed to have settled in nicely and free from that idiot Clemence returning to the the old Donna that everybody loved. Sam busied himself on the general upkeep of the "Jon Jo" supervising the new deck treatment and an overall paint job of the hull. He was resting in the lounge when the call came, 'Mail,' as the letters hit the floor. Two letters from the UK and a large one post marked Virginia. The letter came straight to the point, we have a problem at Fort Bliss, El Paso, Texas, too many patients are dying after being diagnosed as on the mend and healing and as you can imagine the United States Army want to keep the investigation in house and not involve the FBI or any other law enforcement body. Please look into this Sam, the intelligence is contained in the back up registered letter. Sam opened up the letter and read it taking in every detail. The William Beaumont Army Medical Centre Department of Defence Medical facility located in El Paso, Texas have a massive problem, many deaths are occuring on servicemen who have been pronounced fit and well and are in recovery waiting to be returned to there units. No trace of any Barbituate,

Paralytic and Potassium have been found in the blood of the deceased.

Sam departed the next day for El Paso and Bigg's Army airfield located at Fort Bliss. Sam was surprised to see Hercules, Hawk Sprint, Chaparel and Redeye missiles openly displayed with missile crews actively engaged in firing exercises and procedures. He was taken by staff car to the Headquarters in El Paso and introduced to General P.D. Forrester the man responsible for security on the base.

'Colonel Lassiter, welcome,'

'Good to be here sir,' said Sam.

'You understand we want to keep this in house, all hell would break loose if this got to the press,' said the General.

'We'll keep it tight for as long as it is humanly possible, have you anything else for me before I go in knocking heads General,'

'I have an insider a trained nurse Captain Stuart, she is hiding under Lieutenant Tracey Robinson and is based between wards 23a and 25c, these are the general areas where the deaths have been occuring. You are here as a request from the various troop commanders to carry out a series of lectures in jungle warfare, here is your schedule,' said the General handing over the brief to Sam.

'Is there anything I can do for you Colonel,' said the General

'I need a list of all personnel that at some point attend wards 23 through 25 and a copy of there personal file, and a copy of there CV, then I'll get it run through the Pentagon computer, maybe something will be flagged up,' said Sam.

'Call in to my office in the morning Colonel and you will have your information.'

'I've booked you in the doctor's marriage quarters and you will have at your disposal a link to our new device called a RCA Model 501 a transistorized computer, it will help you speed up your search when the information comes from the pentagon.' said the General.

Sam collected a key to his new digs and made his way to Omaha drive and settled himself in. He unpacked and stored his clothes in the built in wardrobes, then sat down with a cup of coffee browsing the list of Doctor's and Head Nurses and there locations. Chief Nurse Colonel L Sheppard name rang a bell for Sam, he wondered if it was the same frumpy Major he rescued from the north Koreans back in 53. Colonel Lucy Sheppard was busy in her office when one of her staff popped in and said,'Colonel, an english Colonel has asked if it was possible to see you, he said he wouldn't take up to much of your time,'

'Ok show him in, I'll see him now,' said Colonel Sheppard.

Sam moved slowly into view and said,

'I see you are still beautiful Lucy Sheppard,'

Colonel Sheppard couldn't believe her eyes and she burst into uncontrolable tears, running across her office and flinging her arms around Sam hugging him so tight. She stayed locked in that embrace for what seemed an age her sobbing gradually subsiding. Her whole staff witnessing this stood up in surprise they had never seen such an action from the normally strict down to earth Colonel.

'Ok everybody back to work,' said a familiar voice,

'Katey Burns as I live and breathe,' said Sam.

'Hello Sam it's good to see you,' said the now Captain Kate Burns.

'I have some prep work to do and I'm sure you guys are busy also, so why don't we get together tonight for dinner I'm buying,' said Sam.

'The officer's mess on campus is ok with me,'said a red eyed Lucy Sheppard.

'8pm I'll be there, bye ladies until tonight,' said Sam turning to leave. Lucy and Kate gave Sam a three way hug as he left the office.

Sam arrived at the Officer's mess and was shown to a table that had been reserved by Colonel Sheppard. Sam was dressed in summer khaki uniform with a chest full of medals which were becoming an embarrassment to him, especially in peace time. Well he could live with that. Both the young ladies arrived looking like movie stars, hair perfect, make up perfect, they really were a pair of fantastic looking women. Sam checked with the ladies and ordered a bottle of chablis and they settled down to a lovely meal.

'Beats MASH food,' said Sam.

'Something you should know Sam, ever since the day we both returned from Doctor Jon's clinic in Tokyo neither of us has been with a man, why I'm telling you this is because you may here some gossip about our relationship,' said Lucy Sheppard.

'I don't give a rats ass what people gossip about Lucy, you are special friends and you always will be,' said Sam.

The meal was completed and after a few drinks they left the mess, and Sam returned to his quarters to study the information from Virginia. After two hours of concentration only one small trivial option caught his eye.

Seven members of the Doctors and Nurses operating out at wards 23 – 25 were of Korean extraction, two doctors, fours nurses, and three pharmacists. Interesting enough for Sam to get a cable off to the General at Virginia and asked for a more detailed search into the seven, even if it meant going to one of the secret agents based in Hanoi.

Sam arranged to meet Lieutenant Robinson in the officer's mess and they immediately got down to business.

'Whatever these morons are using it's damn quick, to quick for the crash teams to recover the patients,' said the Lieutenant. I've checked the Barbituates (Sodium Thiopental), the Paralytic and the Potassium and all the hospital protocol has been adhered too, and none of these chemicals have been prescribed by any of the doctors,' said the Lieutenant,

'So whatever it is comes in through the back door,' said Sam.

Two of the pharmacy nurses lived off base and Sam requested surveillance on both addresses hoping that packages would be received by post.

The post mortem on the latest death was passed on to Sam and it was noted that a minute trace of Succinylcholine (Sux for short} was found in his blood stream. This was serious as Sam clued himself up on the chemical, it was a neuromuscular paralytic drug that stops any breathing and asphyxiates in a matter of seconds.

Sam called a meeting with the General and the Lieutenant.

'This is bad stuff and will be costing an arm and a leg and I'm not sure if any one individual can keep up the payments, so we could have a potential problem with a national,' said Sam,

'Keep up the surveillance on the now three addresses, i'll be here tomorrow same time with some more information that I've requested from Virginia,' said Sam.

The following morning scanned the information from Virginia and found what he was looking for. Doctor Kevin Park entered the USA posing as a South Korean doctor and doctor Amy Field by identical means, Both doctors in fact were North Koreans and had slipped passed American Immigration. They were originally doctor Li Feng and doctor Amy Yang. Sam suggested that the General warmed some asses at Immigration. Two of the pharmacy nurses were North Korea sympathisers and the other a nondescript just along for the ride and a few sashets of cannabis.

'I think we have a connection Feng and Lang were at college together in Hanoi and formed a partnership not only in marriage but to inflict pain on all American's as possible, they recruited sympathisers, Park, Ryu and Lee and began there task to eliminate American servicemen. Every time an American death then it was one for North Korea after the horrendous bombing attacks on there country.' said Sam.

'If we nail the source for the drug drop we can move in and take them down, so high surveillance 24/7.

Sam left the General's office and proceeded to his first lecture with the Strategic Army Corps and the 82nd Airborne Division, it went well although there was nothing new to the presentation, if it works why change the format thought Sam.

Day five and breakthrough day, one of the General's observers firmed up that a package had been delivered to So Yeon Ryu 9.30 am this morning.

'We will watch Ryu you put a tail on the delivery man,' said Sam.

The package was delivered to Doctor Amy Field at 11am.

Sam alerted Lieutenant Robinson in the reception area for wards 23 – 25 as they both waited for doctor Field.

She came into ward 23 calling out orders to the nurses and proceeded towards a bed at the far end of the ward.

'Good morning Private Weeks and how are you today,' she said.

'Looking forward to getting out of here doctor,'

'Sooner rather than later I think Private' she said giving the IV a bit of a shake. She removed the syringe from her pocket and eased the contents into the plastic bag. The curtain was nearly ripped off it's rail as Sam entered the cubicle smashing Doctor Field to the floor and yanking the IV off it's pedestal. All hell broke loose with nurses running everywhere.

'Take it easy everybody this thing here pointing at the bruised doctor Field is responsible for the deaths of 9 American soldiers over the last two months. As the back up arrived the injured Doctor field lashed out at Sam with a scapel causing a large cut on his shoulder, Sam shot her in the knee and she collapsed on the floor in agony.

'Get this bitch out of here,' said Sam to the assembled Military Police. Arrest her husband Doctor Kevin Park and the three pharmacy workers, Park, Ryu and Lee. We will pick up the other two when they come on duty,' said Sam.

'Let me take a look at that arm Colonel it looks nasty,' said a nurse. She took Sam behind a curtain and applied 20 sutures and butterfly clips to the wound and dressed it.

'Sorry to have upset your day ladies,' said Sam to all the other nurses, but we had to get this heap of shit out of here. With the seven now locked up in a El Paso jail, the team was able to direct it's full attention to eliminating the source supplier of the drug. With the help of the El Paso Police Department this was cleared up within two days. Sam completed his final lecture said good bye to his two friends Lucy and Kate and set off back to Santa Barbara with the knowledge that the suppliers of the lethal drug had been arrested and were safely locked away.

CHAPTER 23

Sam returned to Santa Barbara and settled down in the top lounge of the "Jon Jo" resting his throbbing arm. He made an appointment at Santa Barbara General to have his sutres removed. He telephoned Principal Clark ans confirmed that he would be back in harness in the morning.

'I have some news for you Sam,' said Sharon Clark.

'I have received permission from the school Governors to appoint you as a substitute geography teacher, that's of course if you would like that,' she said.

I'd love to give a go, so if you would like to pass the syllabus over to me I'll get studying,' said Sam.

'I'll see you in the morning Sam, have a peep at the UK, you should be ok with that, you can start by telling the class about your own country.' she said. Sam did a bit of prep reading on the UK highlighting specific areas and noted what they were famous for. Staffordshire pottery, Sheffield and Port Talbot for steel production and all the attractions of the capital city of London. Sam had ample information to pass on to forms 2a and 3a, they looked forward to the question and answers at the end of the lesson. The one worry Sam had was that the soccer players grades would not be good enough to get them into college, but now in his new teaching roll he was encouraged to see the improvements.

The court date was set and Monique and her husband stood opposite each other, it was a no contest the guy didn't get a red cent out of the settlement only a dumb skinny blonde.

A registered letter arrived from the General from Virginia three weeks into the term. It read:

Hello Sam, I have received a brief from the Commander of MI5 who has requested our help. The Irish Republican Army (IRA) are receiving millions of dollars from this side of the water, they are not using this money to support families of men imprisoned by the Brits, but being used to purchase ammunition, weapons and explosives. Many British soldiers have been killed. The majority of this money comes from Irish Americans in the Boston area. This goes all the way to Congress as one specific Republican a Peter King of Long Island in fact stayed with the IRA in Northern Ireland and went to a club called the "Felons" who's members were all IRA members. Given the frequency of armed robberies it can be assumed that a large chunk of their income is generated from theft and protection rackets.

Sinn Fein is the political wing of the IRA and is the richest political party in the whole of Ireland. A large portion of these funds originate from the USA through Cairde Sinn Fein. I'll send you a more in depth report with names and locations of the leading IRA fundraisers in the US. What the Brits want us to do is to try and reduce this multi-million dollar payday for these terrorists. Signed General Richards.

After receiving the more compact brief two days later Sam studied the whole thing in great detail. He finally called the General with his thoughts.

'For the first time in a long time General I'm not happy with this mission, it goes to high, National Newspapers, Congressmen, it could be a really hot one,' said Sam.

'I'll do some harassing and give them a frightener but I'm not sure if it's going to do any good, the IRA have got into the minds of the American people that all there donations are to help families whose breadwinners are in prison.'

'Trying to convince these people that the funds are for arms and ammunition is going to be difficult sir,' said Sam.

'I'm not particularly religious sir but one could say that the catholics were not the flavour of the month.'

'I'll do my best General but the stakes are very high in this one and I don't think to much will be accomplished.' said Sam.

'Give it your best shot Colonel,' said General Richards.

Sam was not in a good mood as he boarded the jet for his trip to DC, he sat in his window seat and pondered how the hell he was going to approach the IRA problem. He composed two one page statements that he would leave behind after completing some deterrent activities. Sam read on, the more he new about the conflict the better, it became obvious that the conflict was primarily political but with strong ethnic and sectarian dimensions, it may have seemed so but it was not a religious conflict. Unionists and Loyalists principally protestants considered themselves British and generally want Northern Ireland to remain in the United Kingdom.

The Nationalists and Republicans who were mostly catholics want to leave the United Kingdom and join a United Ireland.

Why the hell don't the British government and Sinn Fein get together for gods sake and at least start talking, thought Sam.

CHAPTER 24

There was a problem at Dullas airport in Washington which resulted in a two hour lay over in Chicago. Sam used this time to compose a couple of "Flyers" which he intended to use after delivering his messages to a member of Congress, the Printer's Union and the student bodies at Washington and Boston. After he had settled into his hotel Sam requested further information from the General.

'I need an appointment with Demercrat Thomas F Johnson in Boston, the top man in the Printer's union in DC and the top people in the students union in both Boston and Washington. Sam needed to get some foundations in place before approaching the many problems.

Sam had a stress free flight to DC and made his way to the Excelsior hotel and waited for the reply from the General.

The following morning a call from the General confirming all the appointments were in place. His first meeting was with the higherarchy of the printer's union.

'Thank you for seeing me gentleman,' Sam began 'World War 2 and later in Korea we fought together and without the support of the USA especially in WW2 we in the UK would now be fluent in German,'

'I'm here to discuss the funding of the Irish Republican Army,' said Sam

'The thousands of American dollars you send to the IRA are not being used to support families of terrorists that are in prison, but to purchase arms, explosives and weapons to kill or maim British soldiers serving in Northern Ireland. None of the funds made available by the Irish Americans ever reach the families that are in need of assistance.' Sam then produced photo's of the carnage caused by the IRA showing death not only to the Brits but to civilians as well.

'You have a Presidential election next November and lets hope the incumbent can use his influence and get the British Government and Sinn Fein to at least sit down at a table and talk.'

'Thank you so much for your time and listening to what I have to say and I hope that you pass on my words to all your members.' Sam placed all his notes in his brief case and left the building.

Sam moved on to address the Student's Union at the George Washington University, the University of Colombia and Georgetown University. He delivered the same message as he did to the Printer's Union and on completion answered every question that came from the floor. Sam stood up and said finally,

'Thank you so much for letting me speak to you and for giving up your leisure time, Before I sit down I have one more thing to say.

'There is a young Senator running for the Presidency next November, his name is Jack Kennedy and he has promised among other things to look into the Northern Ireland situation and use his influence to get the two parties together.' Sam was surprised by the reaction

from the students as they all stood and applauded Sam
as he left the stage.

Sam left Washington after three days of hard work
and flew to Boston Massatusetts to a face to face with
Senator Thomas Johnson.

'Thank you for seeing me sir,' said Sam

Sam went through the whole story leaving out
nothing.

'That's all I have to say sir and thank you for your
time,' said Sam.

Sam rose from his seat and was ready to leave.

'Just a minute young man, what's the hurry,' said the
Senator.

'Your time sir I don't want to overstay my welcome,'
said Sam

'On the contrary I like what you say and I'll bring it
to Congress, it's about time we brought these two
groups together. Thank you and good day to you young
man,' said the Senator rising from his seat and holding
out a hand to Sam.

Sam returned to his hotel really exhausted he was
used to action and not used to talking so much. He
relaxed on the bed and made the call to the Pentagon.

'I'm not sure on how much good I did sir, but I have
tried to put across the truth about what happens to the
many thousands of dollars contributed from Americans
who only know half a story. None of the contributors
are aware of how this money was distributed. They do
now,' said Sam.

'This could be my first real failure in the last dozen
years sir, but in reality the task is a huge problem and
will take a mind change of the American Irish popula-
tion, I have tried to set the wheels in motion with some

of the Trade Unions, the university students union and have the ear of a member of Congress, sorry sir I can do no more,'

'I'm more than happy with your progress in this matter Sam, I'll monitor it closely over the next few weeks and keep you posted.' said the General. Sam boarded the plane for his long flight to LA and after a non eventful flight took the Greyhound to Santa Barbara. Finally an exhausted Sam relaxed aboard the John Jo. He wrote a letter to Lance at Sunningdale informing him that he wouldn't be over for Christmas this year but if invited he would like to come over for six weeks next summer.

CHAPTER 25

Everything had settled down nicely at Goleta Junior High especially after that idiot who upset Donna had been fired. Donna was now back to her normal bubbly self and although still living on the boat was religiously searching for an apartment. Sam had three days to read up on France, Germany for geography and the prohibition period in the USA for history. Satisfied with his prep he fell into a deep sleep, he didn't even make it to his cabin. At 4am he woke up to find that a blanket had been laid over him and a warm female body along side him fast asleep, it was Donna. She felt good beside him so he turned towards her put his arms around her and went back to sleep. Nothing was said by either party as they sat and ate breakfast together in the galley.

Two days later a letter arrived from Lance. Dear Sam, You will find many changes here at the Manor, the whole place has been completely redefined. The estate had become a huge problem to maintain and we were having problems in maintaining the upkeep, in fact we were losing a lot of money. So direct action was needed so we opened the grounds up to the public charging an entrance fee of course and laid on horse riding and lessons.

handled by Katherine, a little fairground with rides for the little ones, buggy rides and a model steam train capable of towing fifty kids and there folks around the perimeter of the estate. We are now a profitable business, thank god. Looking forward to seeing you July/August next year. Lance.

The Christmas term passed and the end of term parties went really well. Sam spent Christmas day with John Li and his family at John's beautiful house and invited them all to come down to Filippo's for Boxing Day. A wonderful meal as usual, then drinks on board with John, Monique, Manuel and family and the bubbly Donna.

The springtime term was well underway when a cable arrived from Virginia. It read:

Hi Sam, Your friends are at it again and getting more powerful as we speak. It appears that the Ku Klux Klan are at it again with a surge of violence against the black residents of Georgia and Alabama. They are bombing schools and churches and the beatings of young black men are becoming far to frequent. The FBI have beefed up there surveillance in the action areas but without much success. They find themselves between a rock and a hard place in dealing with these white supremacists. I'll send on to you a more detailed brief and more comprehensive data.

Two days later a hatfull of information arrived from Virginia identifying the prominent players.

CHAPTER 26

Half term arrived and Sam had ten days to cause havoc to the KKK in Georgia and Alabama. He had an uneventful flight into Atlanta, took a cab to downtown and checked in to a small motel. Sam had taken four different passports, ID's and credit cards on this trip. He decided on Stuart Sullivan for starters. He donned a grey wig and a short well trimmed beard. He decided to take a look around town to familiarise himself and to do a bit of shopping. He went into a store to buy a six pack of budweizer and two bottles of water. He was standing in line at the checkout when he noticed a young teenage girl prancing around in provocative fashion in front of a young black youth. The black kid nodded his head and turned away from her completely ignoring her. She didn't like that at all tore her dress off one shoulder exposing one breast and shouted.

'Momma, Momma he touched me and ripped my dress,' She pointed directly to the young black kid.

'Security arrest that nigger for raping my daughter,' said the mother yelling at the shop security guard. Sam observing all this turned to the woman and said,

'Madam your daughter is a liar,'

'I beg your pardon young man and who the hell are you,' she said.

'It doesn't matter who I am madam your daughter is still a liar,' said Sam.

'She is trying to get the kid into trouble because he didn't respond to her taunting,' said Sam.

A police officer arrived and took statements from the woman, her daughter and Sam, he then escorted the young lad out and took him to a lock up. As Sam turned away he said the woman.

'I hope you are satisfied you have just condemed that young lad to death and all because of a bitch you call a daughter,' said Sam.

'Do you know who I am young man?,' she said

'I don't give a damn who you are madam and your daughter is a spoiled brat and a liar,' said Sam.

'My husband is a prominent member of the Klan and is in fact the Imperial Wizard, I will bring him up to date on this conversation,' she said

'You do that,' said Sam as he left the store.

Sam had parked his hired car just a few cars away from the large black limo that the woman and her daughter had arrived in. As they both exited the store two huge body guards emerged and took the shopping from the woman and guided them both into the car. Sam pulled out making sure that the two jug heads saw him, he pulled out slowly into the traffic and noticed that the limo was following him about three cars back. Perfect thought Sam.

Sam parked outside room 34 and went inside peeped through the blind to see the limo slowly moving off. Sam removed his wig and false beard, washed and changed, walked to the front office and checked out. He then sat in his car hidden away from the motel parking and waited. At around midnight a black sedan came into the motel car park and came to rest outside number 34. Four huge guys emerged from the vehicle each held a baseball bat, they knocked on the door of number 34 and on receiving no reply returned to there vehicle and waited. After an hour the windows of the sedan were opened letting out a lot of smoke. The four guys then settled down and were smoking what looked like weed. Sam gave it another hour to let the dope relax these amateurs, walked over to the sedan and tossed in two high fragmentation grenades with three second fuses through the open car windows.

Sam sprinted for cover behind an adjacent parked vehicle. He then ran to his car and was on the north-bound freeway in 15 minutes.

Sam checked into a motel just on the outskirts of Birmingham Alabama under a new name. He studied the brief from the General one more time and decided to contact the FBI . The Agent in Charge a Tom Nicholson answered the phone.

'Hello, the General said that you would be making contact with me, lets get together and work something out,' said the agent.

'Reserve a table at Mumbo's it's a Thai food place on Forth avenue, say 7.30 this evening,' said Sam.

'I'll see you there,' said Nicholson and replaced the phone.

Sam recognised Tom Nicholson from the photo that the General supplied, they shook hands and sat at a window table.

'I have a man on the inside and he is feeding me a lot of good stuff, he's a bit naive and takes risks and I think that I will have to pull him out of there before he gets found out,'

'I need to meet with your man, I have an idea that could cause all sorts of mayhem for the Klan,' said Sam.

'I'll sort it, I'll be in touch,' the FBI man said.

Sam returned to the motel and switched on the TV and selected a news channel. The news anchorman interupted a weather report. 'I'm sorry Susan he said breaking news, I'll get back to you. Trevor Hughes down in west Birmingham what have you got Trevor,'

'I've got two young black men dangling from nooses, eye witnesses have said it's the work of the Klan. Apparently these two young men have been very active with the black power group,' he said.

'The police are cutting them down now, also I have news of another killing tonight, a young black teenager after being released by the police with no charges against him was assaulted, tied and tethered to a pick up truck and dragged for 2 miles and left for dead, he died in hospital.' said the reporter.

'Ok more on this later,' said the anchor.

Sam had always been a quiet calculating non-panic kind of guy, not letting to much get to him in his chosen occupation. He had lost it only once before and that was in Burma when he discovered the violated bodies of British POWs. He was very angry again, the kid was innocent and didn't deserve to die, some people were going to pay for this big time.

He telephoned Agent Nicholson and requested a quantity of C-4 and some detonators. He also made contact with Tim Sherwood the young agent on the inside and arranged to meet. Young Sherwood drove to the motel and together with Sam put a plan in place. The Klan were planning a mass demonstration in North Birmingham in two days time, there would be Imperial

Wizards attending from different areas of Georgia and Alabama, an expected gathering of 400 Klansmen to watch the ritual burning of the crosses.

At 2am on the morning of the gathering Sam met up with Tim and they set out to a remote barn where the three crosses were laid out ready for the show. Sam pulled off the webbing and sacking back to bare wood and carefully moulded the C-4 into the wood, he inserted small batteries that provide an electrical charge that sets off a tiny explosion in one part of the detonator, this sets off a bigger charge which ignites the payload. When Sam was happy with the result he carefully re-wrapped the sacking and the webbing, putting on an extra wrap and dosing the finished work with paraffin.

'Sam suggested that Tim take time out from Klan watch and return to normal duties for a while as things could get a bit tasty.

Sam checked out of his motel and headed east on the freeway to Atlanta, 146 miles away. He went directly to the airport off hired the rented Ford and headed for departures where he purchased a ticket to Los Angeles under the third ID and passport change. He had four hours to kill before his flight so he sat down with a burger and some fries adjacent to a TV set. After the normal introduction fanfare the news reader shuffling his notes said,

'Breaking news a huge explosion has occurred on the outer limits of Birmingham Alabama, our reporter Jan Sterling has just arrived at the scene, what have you got Jan,'

'This was a Ku Klux Klan rally with around 400 members present, apparently the speeches and chants were made and the crosses set alight, after a few seconds three massive explosions occurred, I can see bodies strewn all over an area of 100 yards, there are many dead and many injured.'

'Ambulances, Police vehicles and Fire Trucks are swarming all over the area, many casualties are being taken to hospital, I'm going to try and get a little closer if the authorities let me, I'll get back to you,'

The news reader continued with other news from the area but was interrupted by Jan Sterling who was interviewing an FBI agent.

'What have we got Agent Harris,' said the reporter.

'We have semtex or C-4 explosives crudely made but effective, we have at this point in time 102 Klan members dead another 100 badly injured, I've never seen carnage like this before in my entire life. I'm purely guessing at this stage but it could be a group of black power flexing there muscles. Sam's flight was called and he settled in his window seat with some doubts in his mind, his feelings of euforia were not right, he must review this situation in depth, he shouldn't be enjoying the killing so much.

CHAPTER 27

Sam arrived back at the boat around midnight, he was a spent force as he sat down at his desk in the top lounge to review his mail. Although he had satisfied himself that he had done a good job on the KKK he was having second thoughts on the carnage he had perpetrated. This was a first for Sam, he had never once questioned a mission or the after effects of his work. His mind became cloudy and full of doubt thinking of the deaths and all the widows and fatherless kids that he had left behind. Maybe enough was enough he thought. He composed a letter to General Richards at the Pentagon:

Dear Sir,

I have been working for you now for the best part of 14 years and for the majority of the time thoroughly enjoying myself ridding the USA of unwanted felons, but the last mission, the KKK thing in Alabama has somewhat altered my perception on things. I've got to get out sir, I have to stop this killing it's getting to me, therefore would you please except this letter as my resignation. I have had many superior officers over the years but I can honestly say that I have the highest regard for you sir and will miss our partnership. Regards Colonel Sam Lassiter.

Sam turned off the lights and strolled slowly to his cabin and collapsed on his bed and slept soundly.

The following morning he rose early posted the letter to Virginia and settled down to read the letters from the UK and to prepare his next weeks geography lessons for 2a and 3a.

He almost missed a note from Principal Clark which as it turned out was very interesting, it was an invitation for middle aged temporary teacher's to qualify as fully fledged teacher's. The courses run from January to January and if the trainee was successful in the examinations they would become fully qualified. Sam completed the questionnaire and posted it off to the Santa Barbara Teacher training College, together with the signing on fee.

Finally he scanned the letters from the UK and read that they were sorry that he wouldn't be over for Christmas, but looked forward to seeing him for a whole six weeks in the summer of 1960. Donna had found a nice guy and she moved out of the "Jon Jo" to join with her new man in a condo overlooking the marina.

Sam spent the next three days preparing lessons and some modified play actions for the soccer teams. On the Friday he received a letter from the training college accepting him on the teacher training course, he would be required to have one full day (Day Release) which would be a Friday and two evening classes a week, Monday and Wednesday. The course would start on Friday 16th January, 1960. Sam thanked Principal Clark for the opportunity of attending teacher training and she confirmed that she would re-schedule Sam's lessons to enable him to attend Fridays lectures. The Christmas term flew by and Sam was enjoying teaching the kids geography and history just as much as soccer periods.

CHAPTER 28

Christmas this year was a sombre affair with Doctor Jon busy sorting out his problems in the Tokyo clinic, Monique with her divorce and Manuel's little lad causing a few problems at school. After giving out his presents Sam wished them all a merry Christmas and left Jon's mansion and returned to the boat. He spent the next week preparing his lessons for next semester and replying to letters from his friends in the UK. He taught his revised schedule for the first week back at school and it seemed to be working out just fine. On the Friday Sam drove his newly acquired Ferrari Dino into the University of California in Santa Barbara and parked it along side a tiny Ford Pinto. He locked up his car looked in the side window of the Pinto and as if being hit with a hammer he saw a lovely looking lady who looked like a twin of Janet. His mind raced as he stared at the young woman.

She wound the window down and said through sorrowful eyes,

'You'll know me next time young man,'

'I'm so sorry for being so rude I had a flash back, you remind me so much of a dear friend of mine, you could be her twin.'

Sam could see that she had been crying and asked,

'Are you ok miss,' said Sam,

'It's an important day for me today I'm enrolling on a teacher's training course and I have had to leave my son with a carer and he was throwing a tantrum when I left home.

'Is the lad poorly or ill,' said Sam,

'He's autistic, it's so sad' she said.'

She gathered her coat and a brief case and started walking to enrolment.

'I'm sorry I stared at you Miss,' said Sam as he followed her into the building. The closer Sam got to her the more she looked like Janet it was uncanny.

The high tiered seats went directly up from the stage of the lecture theatre where the various heads of departments delivered there boring induction briefs. The induction finished at 2pm and the students were told to return to this theatre at 3pm for welcome speeches from the first year instructors. Sam went to the student's cafeteria and picked up a coffee and a bagel, and sat down at a double seated table.

'Hello again,' said the Janet lookalike,

'Hello yourself again young lady, my name is Sam Lassiter and I'm here for teacher training,'

'It looks like you are stuck with me then Sam, I'm on the same course,' she said,

'My name is Susan, Susan Masterson by the way,

'High Susan nice to meet you again, I really am sorry I stared at you but you would never believe how much to look like my friend Janet,' said Sam.

'I'll have to meet her, the way you talk about her she must be very nice,' said Susan,

'She was very nice but unfortunately she died a couple of years ago,' said Sam.

'Oh dear I'm sorry,'

'It's ok' said Sam.

They both wandered back to the lecture room and sat together waiting for the course tutors introduce themselves and set out the programme for the coming year.

At the conclusion of the introductions they both walked to there cars.

'Nice to meet you Susan I'll see you on Tuesday evening maybe we can sit together, with your husbands permission of course,'

'We don't need his permission Sam, he's long gone,'

'What a silly man, see you Tuesday Susan.'

The following Tuesday arrived and Sam was really looking forward to seeing Susan again. Sam arrived early and nabbed a desk towards the back of the classroom. Five minutes later this lovely looking woman appeared, she looked flawless, make up perfect, hair perfect and dressed in a black trouser suit, she paused for a second to scan the room spotted Sam gave him a wave and slid into the desk next to him. Sam hadn't felt that good since watching Janet glide along the arrivals walkway at the New York airport all those years ago. The lead teaching instructor stood and introduced himself along with the other members of the team.

'We have twenty people here to train and we want to know all about you, so five minutes each please, let us all know a little about yourselves,'

After twenty minutes it was Sam's turn, he explained that he fought in WW2 with the British Royal Marines in Burma and reached the rank of Lieutenant Colonel after six years service. He came to the USA in 1946 and worked for the American military doing mostly lectures on Jungle warfare. He lives on a boat in the Santa

Barbara marina, he's single and is looking forward very much to learn the art of teaching. Susan stood up looking very nervous she started by saying that she had intended to teach after she left university but instead got married then pregnant. Her son was born with autism and needed special attention, he is being looked after by a carer while I'm studying here, I just hope I will be able to complete the course and not have to run away to look after him. All the twenty trainees did there thing and the first evening was completed. 'Ok we start in earnest on Thursday evening at 7pm, be early.' said the lead instructor.

Sam walked Susan to her car gave her a little hug and said goodbye. They both climbed into there cars and were gone. Sam did his weekly food shop in Santa Barbara the next day, he also called into a bookshop and purchased two book on autism. If he could help the kid with his anxiety feelings so be it, it would also he hoped bring him closer to Susan. He made himself comfortable and started to read.

Autism is a lifelong developmental disability that effects how a person communicates with, and relates to other people. It also effects how they make sense of the world around them. Some have learning disabilities and need a lifetime of specialist support. They also have an over or under sensibility to sounds, touch, taste, smells, light and colours. Asberger syndrome is part of the autism spectrum. People with Asbergers syndrome are often of average or above average intelligence, but will still have problems understanding and processing language.

They also have difficulties in understanding some of the rules governing social interaction. Sam was deliberately reading very slowly trying to make sure that he understood this very complicated illness. He moved on to anxiety, took out a pen and began to write.

1) Fear of being away from parents.
2) Fear of strangers.
3) Fear of unknown places.
4) Constant crying.
5) Trouble sleeping.
6) Poor appetite.
7) Refusal to go to school.

Sometimes there is no trigger, sometimes a child can feel a general sense of anxiety for no apparent reason, however children usually learn to deal with these fears and overcome anxiety. Sam was now getting very interested and was forging ahead as how to handle these situations. Sam headed up another piece of paper "What to Do" and started writing.

1) Encourage the child to face what they fear.
2) Talk to them about there fears.
3) Ask about what they are thinking and feeling.
4) Gently but firmly explain that there is no need to be afraid.
5) Before moving on to depression Sam researched on what help can doctors give.

The doctor should carry out a physical and phycological examination to determine how serious the anxiety is and then decide the best treatment. The most common drugs supplied are known as SSRIs (Selective Serotonin Reuptake). These take a few weeks to work and after a brief increase in reported anxiety it will reduce. Monitor the child's behavure when first given these drugs. Sam re-read the whole anxiety thing and said to himself that's enough for today, put the book aside, marked the place and would have a look at depression tomorrow. He curled up on the huge sofa, turned on the TV and relaxed. Sam was awake early and dived straight into Doctor Carl Edwards book on autism, he thumbed his way to the chapter on depression and started to read and take notes. Depression consists of feelings of despair and hopelessness and these thoughts last longer than normal feelings. All sorts of reasons can be attributed to this, for instance the loss of a relative, moving to a new place, one of the parents depressed or has a history of bipolar dis1order and frequent sadness. The list of another 10 things that could effect an autistic sufferer were noted by Sam.

So if and when he would meet with master Andrew Masterson, he would be ready.

1) Talk and listen to the child and there concerns.
2) Ensure the child has a healthy diet and a good sleep routine.
3) Take part in regular physical activities.
4) Ensure regular visits to a therapist.
5) Depression can be treated with therapy.

CHAPTER 29

The following Friday Sam pulled in the University car park at exactly the same time as Susan parked up her little Pinto, Sam waited for her to unbuckle, get out of her car and walked with her to lecture room number 7, they sat down next to each other and waited for the lecturer to arrive. Three topics would be discussed todag teaching and learning in action and developing professional practice. The days lesson s finished at 4pm and Sam escorted Susan to her car. Waiting alongside her car was the carer and her young 10 year old son Andrew.

As Andrew threw his arms around his mother, the carer said,

'Andrew has had a bad day Ms. Masterson he has not settled all day,'

When the little lad released his Mum, Sam opened the door of his Ferrari and said,

'What do you think Andrew, do you like her?'

'She is a beaut sir, can I sit in the driver's seat.' said young Andrew.

'Of course you can, If your Mum says ok,' said Sam,

Andrew sat in the driver's seat and started making engine noises and grabbing the steering wheel.

'When you get to know me better we'll go for a ride, with Mother's permission of course,' said Sam,

'Is that a promise mister,'

'Absolutely young man.' helping Andrew out of the low slung sports car.

Susan started the engine of the little Pinto, buckled up Andrew and pulled slowly away out of the car park. Sam waved her down and said,

'Susan your engine sounds a little rough maybe I can give it a bit of a service,' said Sam.

'I've been meaning to get it sorted, I just keep running out of time,' she said.

'Here's my card give me a bell and come on over,' said Sam.

'I'll call you Sam, and thanks.'

Sam was giving the Ferrari a bit of a polish on Sunday morning when the phone rang. He trotted over to the land line a picked up the receiver.

'Hello,' he said,

'Hello Sam it's Susan, I'm having a drive around town with Andrew, doing a bit of shopping. I was wondering if it was possible for you to look at my car, you were right it's making strange noises.

'Bring it on round to the marina and ask the guy on the gate to direct you to the "Jon Jo", and I'll take a look at it,'

'I'll be 20 minutes,' she said.

She eased into one of Sam's reserved parking spaces and got out of the car, she went to the passenger side and helped young Andrew out.

'Hello Mr. Lassiter,' said Andrew

'Hello yourself young man and you can call me Sam,'

Susan looked stunning in a plain white tee shirt and tight blue jeans as she guided Andrew towards Sam.

'Do you two want to go on board and explore the boat, while I take a peep at the Pinto,'

'Can we, can we Mum pleaded Andrew,'

Susan looked questionably towards Sam.

'Go for it I'll need 2 hours at leased to make this little bird sing again,' said Sam.

Sam popped the bonnet of the Pinto and removed all the plugs and cleaned them and putting them back after checking the gaps were correct, he then cleaned and reset the distributor, changed the oil and replaced the rocker gasget. He fired the little engine up and gave the mixture a little twitch and after a minute the motor was running smoothly. Sam wiped the grease from his hands and put some cream on them and made his way across the floating jetty to the Jon Jo. He went into the top lounge to find Andrew fast asleep on the sofa and Susan reading some of Sam's notes on autism.

'You really are a nice man Colonel Lassiter,' she said lifting her head above Sam's printed notes.

'This may seem that I'm hitting on you Susan, but that's not true, yes you are beautiful but I'm afraid way out of my league, but If we are to be friends I need to understand all I can about, anxiety and depression so that I can be friends with Andrew also,'

'Your car is completed and is singing like a bird,' said Sam

'Three things, one, thank you so much for looking at the car, two, thank you for being nice to my son and three, I am not out of your league, believe me.' She rose from the sofa went over to Sam and put her arms around his neck and planted a passionate kiss on his mouth.

'I really want you to be more than a friend Sam, I should go.'

Sam picked up Andrew and carried him to Susan's car and placed him on the rear seat and buckled him up, he turned to the smiling Susan and said,

'See you Monday evening at class,'

'Monday it is,' she whispered and drove away out of the marina.

CHAPTER 30

The following Monday and Wednesday evening classes went well, with special attention given to meeting learners needs and evaluate the effectiveness. Susan during these sessions was really quiet and non-talkative, Sam thought he may have said something that had upset her.

'I'm sorry Sam I've had a worrying two weeks with Andrew, he is not sleeping, his diet is all over the place and he is experiencing stomach pains.

On the day release Friday Sam was just passing Susan's place when he saw the carer standing in the drive with Andrew doubled up and not looking so good. He stopped and called out to Mavis the carer,

'What's wrong with the boy,'

'He has just been violently sick, has a headache and severe stomach cramps,' she said,

'Here's the taxi now, I'm taking him to Santa Barbara General, I've phoned Ms. Masterson,' she said.

'I'll follow you to the hospital,' said Sam.

They arrived at the hospital and Andrew was transferred to a gurney and taken to emergencies. Sam and the carer followed until they were asked to wait while the specialists examined Andrew. Susan arrived looking very pale and went straight to a nurse who told her that her son was in good hands and asked her to sit in the waiting area with Sam and the carer.

'I'm sorry Sam for you missing college today I know how important it is to you,' Said Susan

'There are more important things in life than teaching, Andrew needs as many friends as possible right now,'

After an hour a tired looking doctor emerged through saloon like doors and approached Susan Masterson.

'Ok Ms. Masterson your son has stabilized and is now sleeping soundly, I have prescribed some light drugs for when he has a similar attack.

'You can come and see him now if you wish,'

Susan and the carer went off to see Andrew and left Sam in the waiting room browsing through a magazine.

After half an hour the carer returned to the waiting area and called to Sam.

'Andrew is awake and he wants to see you,'

Sam entered the single room where he found Andrew sitting up in bed with a huge smile on his face and a weary looking Susan sitting close by the bed.

'You are looking wonderful young man, you look as fit as a flea,'

'The doctor has told me that they are keeping you in overnight just to make sure that you are ok, are you ok with that?'

'I'm ok with that Sam as long as I can have a ride in your car tomorrow,'

'You've got a deal,' said Sam offering a closed fist to the youngster who returned the soft punch.

Susan told the carer to take her car back to her home and relax for the day, while she sat with Andrew. Sam volunteered to spell Susan, in fact Andrew insisted on it.

At around 10 pm Andrew was out for the count so Sam drove Susan home and then retuned to his boat.

CHAPTER 31

On the Saturday morning Sam arrived early at the hospital to find Andrew in fine spirits he had been told that he could go home today. Susan arrived with a clean set of clothes for Andrew and after signing his release they left the hospital. Sam had already taken a cushion from his lounge so that he could prop up Andrew In the Ferrari. He sat Andrew in the front seat and buckled him in and took off in the direction of Susan's apartent. He drove around for an hour and Andrew loved every minute of it. Sam noticed that Andrew's concentration levels were slipping and he was losing energy, so he drove into a burger place so that Andrew could rest.

'I think it's a good time for you to have a little sleep, I'll take you home and tomorrow we can go for a swim, what do you say about that?'

'I'm not to good in the water, but I'll give it a go,' said Andrew

'So ask your Mum if it's ok and we'll do it,' said Sam.

On Sunday morning Sam dressed in his shorts and tee shirt was sitting under a giant parasol drinking a cup of coffee when Susan pulled into the marina and made her way over to the swimming pool towards Sam. Andrew sprinted ahead of her and jumped into the arms of Sam. Sam bought some drinks a coke for Andrew and a fizzy water for Susan. As he passed her the drink he took a long look at her, blonde hair tied in a pony tail, beautiful face with a faint trace of make up, long slender brown legs, and a smile to die for, she not only looked like Janet she was the same between the ears, a really nice person. Sam helped Andrew take off his shirt and then put him squealing under his arm and trotted off to the tiny pool alongside the main olympic sized pool. He started off with his arm bands on and then graduated to not needing them.

'Push out and blow Andrew you are doing great,' said Sam, as Andrew was overcoming fast his fear of water. Susan then stepped into the pool in a tiny pink bikini, splashed Sam and Andrew and then ran out of the pool before they could retaliate.

'We'll remember that won't we Andrew,'

'Yes we will, we'll remember that mummy,'

'Ok, before we have ice cream, I think you are ready for the big pool, how do you feel about that Andrew,'

Much to the apprehension of Susan, Sam and Andrew waded into the shallow end of the pool. Sam one side and Andrew the other.

'Lets go Andrew swim over to me, if you find yourself sinking hold your breath and keep going, a mouthful of water isn't going to hurt you,'

Andrew went under once on his trip across the width of the pool but just like he was told he kept going and made it across into the safe arms of Sam.

Tears were streaming from Susan's eyes when she saw the elation on Andrews face.

'I'm so proud of you,'

The three of them were engaged in a bear hug, Sam had never seen them so happy. 'There is a swimming coach here at the marina, I'll call him and arrange for Andrew to receive his first swimming certificate.'

'Lets get some lunch, do you think your son deserves ice cream for seconds,' said Sam directing his comments to Susan.

'Yes, Yes he does,' said Andrew.

Sam didn't want to be seen as taking over so he phrased his next comments accordingly.

'Do you want a ride in the Ferrari this afternoon Andrew?, if yes we need you to have a little rest now, don't forget you have just come out of hospital, isn't that right Mum,' said Sam.

Sam made sure that Andrew was comfortable on the huge L shaped sofa and that Susan was ok, he went down to the galley and prepared some salad for lunch. He then returned to the top deck lounge to find both Susan and Andrew fast asleep, he covered them both and then made his way over to his desk to try and complete the reports for the forthcoming PTA evening. Sam didn't write the usual drivel that formed most of the reports, but dug deeper and called it how it was, this didn't go down to well with some of the old school, but highlighting the kids shortfalls he hoped would spur them on to do better. He had put in a good hour and was pleased with the progress with only around 50 to complete.

Andrew was still sound asleep but Susan was waking, she sat up wiped her eyes and gave her hair a bit of a flick, walked over to Sam's desk.

'We have a big half term PTA gig at the school next Wednesday, where I see all the parents and let them know how there kids are getting along, that's only 2a, 3a and 2 and 3b, which means I have 120 comments to make on there reports,' said Sam tidying up the papers on his desk and moving over to the sofa where Susan joined him.

'I really can't believe how quickly we have become friends and how my son loves your company, I consider myself a lucky girl,'

'I don't get much chance with the ladies I seem to be either teaching or coaching or going to college.'

'Well Sam Lassiter you've got a chance now with me, I think you are a lovely man and cute with it,' she said.

Sam moved closer to her and she put both her arms around his neck, Sam pulled her towards him and kissed her passionately both tongues working overtime. They held on to each other for what seemed a lifetime and only separated when Andrew began stirring.

'Everybody up for salad,' said Sam rising and making his way to the galley.

'I'll be back in 5 minutes,'

The three of them sat down and ate the salad, had a fruit juice and watched a TV for a while.

'Who wants a ride in a Ferrari,' said Sam.

'Me,' said Andrew jumping up from the sofa and grabbing a cushion.

'I'll see you in a half hour Susan why don't you explore the boat.

Sam and Andrew had a great ride, taking in Goleta Junior High, the local football stadium and the University of California Campus in Santa Barbara. Sam returned to the boat to find Susan waiting at Filippo's drinking some wonderful smelling coffee.

'Time to go home Andrew,' she said.

'I want to stay here with Sam, I don't want to go home,' he said going over to Sam and grabbing him around the waist.'

'You young man have been absolutely fantastic today, swimming without your armbands well enough to achieve your first certificate, getting some study reading in, and behaving like a well mannered gentleman all day. Now I think that you may want to come over again and as you are my new best friend you would be welcome, but you must go now take your meds and have a lovely sleep so that when you return to the "Jon Jo" you can once again enjoy yourself. Is that fair,' said Sam.

'That's fair,' said the youngster.'

'Good bye then Andrew see you soon,'

Susan nodded her approval and led her boy to her car, she gave Sam a peck on the cheek and said that she would see him on Monday evening in class. Sam watched as the Pinto pulled out of the marina and turned right towards the north side of Santa Barbara.

At evening class on the Monday night the main topic was exploring teaching and learning and the ability to share their professional learning with collegues,

'Finally ladies and gentle men this Wednesday we won't be here, we have been invited to attend a parent/teachers evening at Goleta Junior High, where we can see our Mr. Lassiter in action, these meetings are of great benefit to the teacher, parent and the student. I'm not sure how good our Mr. Lassiter is, but we will find out on Wednesday.

Sam was walking Susan back to her car, when a tall gangly guy emerged from between two vehicles.

'Hello Susan, lovely to see you,' he said. Giving her a hug and peck on the cheek.

'Hello Martin what are you doing here, I thought you were in New York,'

'I've changed mind I want you to be part of my life again, I made a big mistake and I want you back,' said Martin Masterson.

'I think it is time for me to leave Susan, I'll see you on Wednesday,' he said making his way to his Ferrari.

'Don't go Sam,' she said, but it was to late as Sam was already out of ear shot.

'My life has changed since you flew off to New York, Andrew has settled and I'm back at college to complete my training to teach again,'

'Give me a chance again Susan, I'll prove to you that I really mean it,'

'I can't promise, lets go for a drink and talk about it,' said Susan.

Wednesday was different as all the student teacher's gathered for an introduction to Goleta Junior High by Principal Clark.

Oh, one more thing don't be to hard on your fellow student Mr. Lassiter because around here he is well loved by parents and students.

Sam went over to his desk for the evening and started the interviews with the children from 2a and 2b. The trainee teacher's came and sat down on Sam's side of the desk and watched his technique. Sam's way of doing things was direct and to the point, no icing on the cake unless it was earned. Sam finished his talks with the juniors and moved on to 3a and 3b, and for the first time that evening Susan moved into the seat beside him. Sam nodded and smiled.

Mrs. Martinez and son Arturo were up next and were both greeted with a large hug, which surprised all the student teacher's in the immediate proximity.

'You remember I asked for an improvement in his school work to accompany his excellence on the sports field, well Arturo you did it and I'm very proud of you well done, keep this standard and I can see no reason that a scholarship wouldn't be granted. At around 9pm the proceedings came to an end and all the student teacher's collected in the gym for coffee and cookies.

Sam was standing in a small party in the centre of the gym with Principal Clark and Henry Mason the head lecturer of the teacher training college and were engaged in what seemed to be a serious conversation.

'I have my own way of writing these reports sir, I believe the kids and the parents need to know the truth and I also believe they can be used as a motivator, I see no point in beating around the bush, so I write the truth. Both the Principal and the lecturer were in agreement with this. Principal Clark thanked all the teacher's for a great PTA and hoped it was beneficial to the trainee teacher students. Everybody left to go home Sam did not seek out Susan and just drove straight back to the marina.

Sam was met at the security gate by old Tim the gate man.

'I've got a visitor for you Mr. Lassiter he's in my cabin, he insists on seeing you,'

Sam entered Tim's little cabin to find a tearful Andrew sitting close to Tim's stove trying to keep warm.'

'What the devil are you doing here Andrew, your mother will be worried sick,'

'No she won't and I hate the man who is at our house now, I hate him, I hate him,' he sobbed.

Sam and Andrew made there way over to the boat and Sam settled .the lad down on the sofa, made him a hot drink. He made the call to Susan's number and a guy answered the phone.

'Let me talk to Susan please, it's Sam Lassiter,'

'Can I help,' said Martin Masterson,

'What part of can I speak to Susan don't you understand,' said Sam.

There was a short pause and Susan was on the line.

'I have a huge problem Andrew has run away and I don't know where he is, I'm sorry to be so blunt but I am worried sick, so really I have no time to talk to you Sam.'

'Andrew is safe and he is with me on the Jon Jo, he is safe, warm and fed, all he wants is to see you, so maybe you could come over. It would be good if you come on your own, if he meets your man Martin it could well spark off another anxiety attack,'

'Thank you so much Sam, I'm on my way.

Susan arrived at the marina and dashed up the gang plank and went aboard the Jon Jo, she found Andrew asleep on the large sofa.

'Is he ok Sam, he's never done anything like this before,'

'He's as safe as houses here, quiet and stress free, I'm not trying to put your friend Martin down here, but the lad seems to have a problem with him,'

'A huge problem Sam, you should have heard his comments after I had put the phone down from your call. He has no idea what autism is all about, he said that the lad needs a good hiding and a slap around the head to drive some sense into him,'

'I'm sorry Susan the guy is your friend but I'm afraid he comes across as an idiot,' said Sam.

'He is no longer a part of my life past, present or future, I still can't believe he turned up after over a year away and expected me to welcome him with open arms. I've sent him packing he is well out of my life,' said Susan.

'You are welcome to stay here overnight, I think it's best we let the little fella rest,' said Sam.

Susan made a phone call to a distressed carer and told her not to worry and that Andrew was fine and in good hands, she also confirmed that Martin had left her apartment.

'I'll be staying with Andrew on board Sam's boat overnight and I'll see you first thing in the morning.' Susan said to her carer.

Sam collected a pillow and a duvet and laid it out on the sofa adjacent to where Andrew was sleeping.

'You should be nice and comfortable, I prefer the sofa to my bed,' said Sam,

'Would you like something to eat or a drink?' said Sam.

'A nice martini would hit the spot Sam,'

'One Sam Lassiter special martini coming up,' as he made his way over to the bar.

'Didn't get much time to pack a few items, especially a night shirt, can I borrow one of yours,'

Sam prepared an extra dry martini for Susan and placed it on the coffee table, he then went to his cabin and selected a shirt for Susan. She took it and said thanks and used the toilet to change into her borrowed night wear.

She returned to the top lounge and sat on the sofa the shirt riding up and exposing her sun tanned thighs, as she slowly sipped her drink. Sam left for his cabin and changed into shorts and a T shirt his normal sleeping gear. He returned to the lounge and said his good nights.

Susan was curled up on the sofa with just her head protruding over the duvet when she said,

'Stay with me tonight Sam,' and opened up the duvet to allow Sam to slip in beside her.

It didn't take long for Sam to rise to the occasion as he pulled the lovely Susan closer.

'Sorry about the hard on, you do realise that you are a very beautiful woman and if I didn't rise to the occasion I could be cast as a queer.'

Her only reaction was to pull him even closer and move her hips to feel the full benefit of his hardness.

'There will be times when we can make love the whole night, but here and now is not the right time, try and get some sleep,' said Sam.

The following morning Sam washed and changed, left a note to the soundly sleeping Susan to the effect that she and her son could stay on board for as long as she liked.

The geography lessons with 2a and 3a went well, taking in all the great mountains of the world and there location, from Ben Nevis in Wales to Everest in Nepal and K2 on the China Pakistan border.

At lunchtime he phoned Susan to see if she and the boy were ok.

'We are fine thanks Sam and would like to stay with you for a few days, it will also give my carer a bit of a rest,'

'You are absolutely welcome, I'll see you about 6pm.' said Sam.

As Sam had a free period in the afternoon he phoned Doctor Jon.

'Jon it's Sam, a question who do you know in Santa Barbara general who specialises in autism?'

'I have a colleague who is the number 1 in California for this dreadful disease, but he is very expensive,' said Jon.

'I need to talk to the man to arrange for him to see a friend of mind's son, the kid is just 10 years old,' said Sam.

'I'll get him or one of his minions to give you a call so that you can arrange an appointment,'

'Thanks Jon, you're the man.'.

When Sam arrived at the boat after work he was greeted by Andrew who grabbed his hand and led him off to the galley where Susan was preparing a great smelling lasagne. Sam greeted Susan with a little kiss on her cheek and then selected a bottle of chablis from the wine rack, which he removed and placed in the fridge. What could be better than this Sam thought as he sat down at the table in the galley with his little friend Andrew and the beautiful Susan.

Sam suggested that they both adjourn to the upper lounge so that Susan could help with Andrew's home-work and that he would tend to the washing up. Fifteen minutes later Sam joined them, he arrive in the middle of an argument.

'I tell you Mum it was William Caxton who invented the printing press not some printer from Atlanta, Sam you tell my Mum,'

'Sorry Susan wonder child is right good old Bill was the inventor, it was slap in the middle of the British industrial revolution in the 19th century,' said Sam.

'How do you like school Andrew,' said Sam.

'It's ok sometimes, I don't think the teacher knows where I'm coming from, sometimes my answers seem to be right for me but they tend to confuse the teacher,'

'Well I think you are a very clever young gentleman with every possibility of going to college,' said Sam.

'Now Einstein it's ready for bed,' said Sam.

Sam relaxed as Susan put Andrew to bed in the rear birth, he reviewed the weekly local teacher's brief to see if Goleta High had any stories, which they didn't.

Susan returned and flopped onto the sofa next to Sam. The nearness of this beautiful looking woman made Sam reminisce of the distant Janet days.

'How do you feel about sending Andrew to a special school where the only students are autistic and the teaching staff are all trained in dealing with the disease,'

'I have my doubt's, my worry would be bringing on a depression attack you know autistic kids don't like moving to a different place, but if we could get over that hurdle, yes I would love for him to go to such a college, but I have only a few dollars saved for rainy day and wouldn't be able to afford it anyway,' said Susan.

'Susan I have friends in high places in the medical field and will be talking to the top consultant for treating autism, my doctor friend Jon says that he is the best in California. I would like you and Andrew to go and see him, what do you think?'

'That would be wonderful, thank you so much,' she launched herself on Sam pinning him to the sofa and planted a huge kiss on his mouth. They stayed locked together for what seemed to be an age there bodies close and intimate.

'I want you to make love to me Sam,'

Sam undid the buttons on her shirt and eased her ample breasts out and removed her bra, and as Sam took off his shirt she slid off her skirt. Sam struggled to get off his trousers and had that terrible thought again about finishing before he started. He need not have worried, the cool Susan made all the right moves, taking things slowly at first with passionate kissing that went on for an age and then taking a grip of Sam's rock hard penis and gently caressed it. She then lowered herself and took the whole of his penis into her mouth going up and down his shaft and occasionally using her tongue.

Sam eased her off his penis and kissed her nipples until she was hot to trot, he removed her tiny panties and slid his erect penis inside Susan. They made love for about a half an hour and it was wonderful, the two bodies Sam's rugged muscled frame and Susan's toned body locked together in perfect harmony.

Sam rose early the following morning, left a note for Susan saying that a Doctor Mark Kramer would be making contact with her on her home telephone today to arrange for an appointment for Andrew and yourself.

The school day was strictly routine for Sam as he practiced some of the techniques learned at college. The kids especially 3a had a habit of cleverly switching it around so that Sam was talking about his exploits in Burma during WW2, cheeky buggers thought Sam.

Sam arrived back at the boat around 6pm and immediately phoned Susan.

'Yes we have an appointment with Doctor Kramer next Monday at 3pm, after our interview he will take us around the school and we can ask as many questions as we like, he comes across as a lovely man. I'll get the carer Maria to come over and pick up Andrew, so if you could drive me home after class that would be great,'

'Not a problem, see you tomorrow,' said Sam.

Susan arrived a little late at evening class on the Wednesday night, apologised to the lecturer and made her way to the desk next to Sam, who whispered the page number in the notes which were being reviewed. The lecturer raised his hand to get attention and said,'

'I want you all to look at this report and lets pull it to bits if we can, 'he placed the report on a machine and zoomed it up on the screen Sam recognised the report it was one of his, but with the teacher's name blotted out. He waited for it to be slaughtered.

'Beverley what do you think?'

'Sorry sir I can't find anything wrong with it,' she said sitting down.

'Daniel what about you,'

'Me too, I'd like my reports to read like that one,' he said pointing to the screen.

'And what about you Mr. Lassiter,' said Ken Smales the lecturer.

'It's not bad, it's one of mine, I tried to take the sharp edge off a tad because the lad is a quiet unassuming lad and wouldn't react to well to stinging criticism. Some pupils you can hit hard, what it's really about is knowing your students and using words that will enhance improvement. I was fed up when I was in school when I read the comment "Could do better", I hated it.'

'I try to make my reports individual and not generalise, I make copious notes throughout the term and refer to these notes at report time. This is hard work and time consuming and a lot of late nights, I intend to carry on using this system unless of course Mr. Smales tells me different,' said Sam.

'Mr. Smales says don't change a thing.'

'This report will be added to our brief on reporting and used as a standard that we require.'

He arrived back at the boat around 6pm and phoned Susan immediately and she confirmed that she and Andrew have an appointment with Doctor Kramer next Monday at 3pm.

'I'll get Maria my carer to drop me off at evening class, so if you can take me home it would be great,'

'Not a problem, see you tomorrow,' said Sam.

Susan arrived a little late at evening class, made her apologies to the lecturer and sat down alongside Sam.

'Ok lets take a break,' said the Ken.

'Sam, Doctor Kramer is a wonderful man Andrew took to him right at the get go, he took us all around the private school that was situated in beautiful surroundings to see if we both liked it. The only thing that worried Susan was the fees which are expensive and she mentioned this to the Doctor.

'I receive a grant every year from the California State which allows me to take in an additional two students and I would like one to be Andrew,' said Doctor Kramer.

'What do you think Andrew do you want to come here,'

'I would love to,' said Andrew.

'Lets sign up Doctor, this is a chance in a lifetime,' said Susan.

The bell sounded at 9pm and the students made there way out to there cars carrying wads of homework to complete on encouraging and support innovation and collaboration.

'I'll see you on Friday I'll call for you if you like,' said Sam.

'Lovely see you then Sam,' she said giving him a peck on the cheek.

Friday came and went quickly and smoothly and before he new it Sam was back at the boat preparing for next weeks lessons and his soccer training schedules.

CHAPTER 32

It was a normal active Monday morning for the majority of the teacher's but mid morning for Sam meant a quick coffee in the staff room before 2a geography.

There were three other staff members sitting quietly drinking there coffee when two small calibre shots rang out.

'What the hell was that,' said one of the teacher's

'Sounds like a 38,' said Sam rushing out of the staff room and bumping in to two students.

'What's going on Gary Symonds,' said Sam.

'A coloured guy has a pistol and he's fired a couple of shots into the ceiling, he's holding two girls at gun point in Miss Nugent's class in 4a, he's really pissed,' said the lad.

Sam entered 4a and saw instant relief on some of the students faces. Sam recognised Joseph Lorrenzo senior who was standing at the front of the class with what looked like a Saturday night special 38 Smith and Wesson, which was pointed in the general direction of the two whimpering girls, who stood motionless, petrified.

'What's going on Joe,' said Sam,

'Coach Lassiter these two white bitches have managed to get my son Joe suspended by telling a bunch of lies to

Principal Clark, they said that he touched there tits and fondled there asses, all this is untrue, my boy does not fraternise with white girls he has a steady girlfriend, he was set up coach,'

Sam noticed that Joe's thumb was twitching and flicking the safety catch on and off, and if he could get the timing right could releave him of the weapon.

'This isn't the way to do it Joe, let the Governors and Principal Clark get it sorted before anybody gets hurt,' said Sam.

'If these young ladies are lying, then young Joe will be reinstated.' Joseph pointed the 38 in the direction of the two girls.

'Why did you tell these lies about my boy you have ruined his chances of going to college,' he said.

'We don't like the way he struts around the place like he is some kind of god, so we thought we would bring him back to earth by spreading a rumour,'

'Not a particularly clever thing to do, you could well have scuppered his chances of getting into college, with these stupid remarks, you have been very silly and juvenile,' said Sam.

'Ok you heard them Joseph put the gun down on the floor,' said Sam.

Joseph senior placed the 38 on the floor and sat down at Miss Nugent's desk hands on his head and crying,

Sam went over to him and put a reassuring arm around his shoulder. The Police arrived read Joseph his rights, cuffed him and took him away. The two girls together with a few of class 4a were taken care of by the Santa Barbara ambulance medics.

Sam looked around the classroom and helped a frail looking Miss Nugent to her feet and asked her if she was ok to carry on teaching.

'Give me a half an hour Sam and I'll be ok,' she said

'Ok 4a take a half hour break and then be back in your seats,' said Sam.

'Are all you guys ok?' said Sam.'

A chorus of yes came back from the class.

Principal Clark entered the classroom and said,

'If any student wants to take the rest of the day off they can, but make sure you are in bright and early tomorrow morning,'

'Sam, my office please,' said Sharon Clark,

'What the hell were you doing going into a room with a guy pointing a gun at your head,'

'Sharon my job away from teaching when I'm working for the US government is sometimes of a violent nature and I'm quite used to knives and guns being pointed in my direction. In this case Joseph Lorrenzo for the majority of the time had the safety engaged, so damage limitation,'

'Although I don't like my staff putting themselves in danger thank you so much for your brave effort, if somebody had been hurt the school would have been castigated and threatened with closure,'

'When is the hearing for young Joe,'

'Thursday 2pm, do you want to be called,'

'Yes please Ma'am, I may be able to help young Joe, but I'm not so sure about my friend Joe senior, he could be in a whole lot of trouble,'

In the afternoon Sam strolled along to Miss Nugent's class and asked if he could say a few words.

'Of course you can Mr. Lassiter,' said Emily Nugent.

'I'd just like to say how brave you guys and your teacher were this morning, you are all a credit to Goleta Junior High, well done,' Sam turned and left the classroom.

CHAPTER 33

At the Monday evening class the fracas at Goleta Junior High was brought up for discussion and the class debated the "Fors" and the "Against's" in the matter, with the consensus of opinion that they could understand the father's wrath, but not for him to go in waving a gun around.

'You see how careful we have to be in our jobs, I'm not sure you should have entered the classroom like you did Mr.Lassiter,'

'Neither was I sir,' said Sam.

After a brief silence the lecturer said that the main thrust of this evenings class was 'How does a mentor share knowledge and perspective to develop the growth of a teacher'.

Before dropping Susan off at her apartment Sam took her to a little bar for a night cap.

'You were either very brave or very silly to confront that gentleman head on especially with him holding a weapon, please promise me you won't do it again,' said Susan

'I can't promise that Susan, but I'll take care, see you on Wednesday, I'll call for you,' said Sam.

Wednesday's lecture was entitled 'Presentation and a proposal of developing professional practice'.

Sam dropped Susan off at her apartment and excused himself saying that he had to prepare himself for young Joe's Governor's hearing tomorrow.

The hearing began right on time at 2pm and a very nervous Miss Nugent was first up. She had rehearsed well and informed the board that Joe Lorrenzo Jr. was a straight A's student and a pleasure to teach and before this unfortunate hearing was destined for a position in a major college.

Sam was writing a few notes outside the Principal's office when he was called.

'What's your take on this Mr. Lassiter,' said the chairman heading up the enquiry.

'I can honestly say that the young man has always been an excellent example of how to conduct himself both on and off of the sports field. The only contact I have with Joe Lorrenzo is for sports and as I have said he conducts himself as a gentleman.'

'Ok, thank you Mr. Lassiter,'

The two girls were then interviewed separately and amid tears and sobs said that they had made the whole thing up just to get at Joe's girl friend Billie Jean Lockyer. The two distressed girls were led away in disgrace and met by two sets of very irate parent's.

'Call Joe Lorrenzo Junior,' said the leader of the disiplinary panel.

'It looks like you have been badly wronged young man and we the Governor's of Goleta High offer our extreme apologies and we would like you to continue your studies with us until you graduate to college, what do you think young man?'

'Thank you sir, I'll do my best to get back into the swing of things, I could have a problem confronting the two young ladies as they are in the same set as me, but I can make it work here at Goleta, my only big worry is not for me sir, it's for my Dad, he's up in court next Friday.

'We wish you all the best with that, I have suggested to both of the girls parents that it would be a good idea for them to make a fresh start in another school, and they have agreed to this,'

'That's fine I'll complete my schooling at Goleta.' said Joe.

Day release went well on Friday and Sam enjoyed the debate on dealing out punishment to obnoxious students.

Susan spent the whole week end establishing Andrew's new home, which fortunately he took to like a duck to water, Susan was aware that moving an autistic child can cause a problem.

The following Monday Sam was summoned to court for the Joseph Lorrenzo hearing. Sam was called and took the oath.

'Mr. Lassiter please tell us the sequence of events on that Monday morning,' said the defending lawyer.

'At around 10am on that Monday morning I was in the teacher's staff room drinking coffee with three other teacher's when we heard what sounded like small arms fire, clearly hearing two shots, I raced out of the staff room to be met by two students sprinting away from 4a Miss Nugent's class.

'What's going on in 4a Simpson,' said Sam

'Joe Lorrenzo's dad was holding two girls at gun point and issuing threats, he fired two shots into the ceiling bringing down a white powder covering desks and some pupils. I entered the classroom and approached Joe senior.

'What the hell are you doing Joe,' I said,

'These two bitches are telling lies and are crucifying my boy, they said he touched there tits and fondled there asses. This is a lie, my boy does not go anywhere near white girls, he has a beautiful black girl friend and has no need to flirt with these girls, what they have done is ruin his chances of going to college by telling lies,'

Sam keeping his eye on Joe seniors itchy trigger finger, looked at the girls and said,

'Well I said to the two girls what's your story,' One of the two girls said through a flood of tears that they both tried to get Joe Lorrenzo into trouble because he didn't fancy either of us and we were jealous of his black bitch.

I then told them to watch there mouth.

'I then changed my focus towards Mr. Lorrenzo and noticed that his thumb was playing nervously on the safety of the 38, and a thought of taking the gun away from him. But decided not to try this as many of the class students were in the shooting area.

'Ok Joe you heard it from the girls it's time to put the gun down before anybody gets hurt,' I said

Then Joe in frustration fired a shot through the classroom window and dropped the 38 on to the floor, he then came over to me and embraced me, he then said I'm so sorry Sam. It's ok Joe I said, now go along with the officer's who had just entered the classroom. The two officers from SBPD read the miranda to Joe, cuffed him and led him away to a waiting police car.

'You two young ladies go to the ambulance medics in the playground and let them sort you out and I suggest you call your parents and take the rest of the day off,' said Sam

'That's about it, your honour,' said Sam.

'Your witness,'

Miss Rachel Shearing stood looking almost perfection, tall, and elegant in an Armani suit and expensive shoes.

'Mr, Lassiter you are an unqualified substitute teacher at Goleta High is that correct,' she said

'Objection your honour demeaning,' said the defence lawyer,

'Sustained, be careful Miss Shearing you don't want to get on the wrong side of me,' said Judge Anderson.

'Sorry your honour, when did you become a expert on small arm weapons Mr. Lassiter is this part of your brief at Goleta High, or maybe that's how you got the job,' she said with a sneer.

'Objection your honour,'

'Last warning Miss Shearing, be careful,'

'It's ok your honour I'll answer those questions,' said Sam

'What my teaching credentials are to do with this case is beyond me, but yes at this moment in time I am a substitute teacher, but in 18 months time I will be fully qualified. As far as me being an expert on weapons let me run this across you. Between 1940 and 1945 I was in the British Royal Marines, 44 Commando stationed in Burma fighting the Japanese, so you must believe I had a fair knowledge of weapons. So the weapon fired by Mr. Lorrenzo was a Smith and Wesson snub nosed 38 derived from the original 38 the Detective special, it has a 2" barrel, and delivers a 130 grain full metal jacket bullet, a bullet diameter of 9.6 mm, loaded at 13000 pounds per square inch, and a muzzle velocity of 725 feet per second. So madam am I an expert on weapons, in a word, yes'.

There was a long pause the prosecuting lawyer fumbling her paperwork and trying to regain her position.

'So you condone Mr. Lorrenzo's waving around and firing a weapon Mr. Lassiter,'

'Of course I don't condone it, Mr. Lorrenzo was stupid to do what he did, I'm so pleased only pride was hurt and that nobody got shot. I've thought a lot over the last few days about what I would have done if my sons future was ruined by two ladies who told lies, maybe I would have done the same as Joe Lorrenzo senior,'

'No further questions your honour,'

The jury was out for only half an hour.

'Have you reached a verdict,' asked,Judge Anderson

'Yes your honour, we have a majority decision, we find Mr. Lorrenzo guilty of firing an unlicensed weapon in a crowded area that could have caused injury or death, but with mitigating circumstances.

'My decision is this Mr. Lorrenzo you will carry out 300 hours of community work in the Santa Barbara area, you will not be permitted to hold a license for a weapon and you will report to a probation officer on a daily basis. The reason for such a lenient sentence is because you are the only breadwinner in the Lorrenzo household, so don't let me down,' said the judge with a smile.

Sam and the two Joe's along with his other younger son Ike hugged each other in the courtroom with tears of happiness.

Over the next few weeks things settled back to normal at school with the Lorrenzo affair just a bad dream, and the teacher training falling back into a nice rhythm. It was becoming obvious that Susan and Sam were becoming an item, when they were together it was difficult to get a cigarette paper between them. For the first time since Janet, Sam thought he might be falling in love.

Back on board Sam was sorting through his mail when he caught site of a letter from Virginia which did not bear the official Pentagon envelope. It was from his old mentor General Richards, who related that he was now retired and living in West Virginia establishing a thoroughbred horse breeding ranch. He invited Sam down to the ranch and maybe talk of old times. He also said that he had given Sam's name to the new man in charge a General Clyde Peterson in case you may want to make a come back. Come down and see me Sam, it will be great.

CHAPTER 34

A letter arrived the following morning from a General Clyde Peterson at the pentagon, he introduced himself and said that he had taken over from General Richards. He was aware that you are taking time out from any missions and that if and when you did return it would be on a part time basis utilising Christmas, Easter, summer holidays and the various half terms. This timing would not jeopardize his teaching duties. I have a problem Sam your friends the Russian Mafia are at it again in Las Vegas, they are moving in on mob controlled areas and it looks like a blood bath waiting to happen. I have lost three agents, the LVPD has lost 2 detectives and the FBI insider has just been found dead in the desert. He managed to get a message out to us before his cover was blown.

A woman assassin known as Karen Clayton known to us as Katrina Politoff is the assassin her cover is the Manager of the Golden Nugget Hotel in Vegas. So she has taken out six good people, incidentally when she completed her murders she cut off the men's penis's and severed the one girl agents breasts, so you can see she's quite a lady. She and her four bodyguards need to be taken out Sam, please let me know by return if you want a piece of this. He signed it Clyde Peterson.

Sam hated the Russian Mafia for what they did to his friends on LAPD a couple of years back and although he should decline the mission his hate for the Russians won the day. He accepted the mission and would stand by for the more extensive intel.

This information arrived two days later and Sam spent a long time reviewing it. He was to travel to Los Angeles and meet up with his wife to be for two weeks at the Excelsior Bus Company, they would travel together with a bus load of holiday makers to Las Vegas and stay in the Golden Nugget Saloon on the strip. He met his wife to be for the next two weeks, a tall attractive woman about 28 to 30 years old, she introduced herself as Fay Sheppard.

'Hello Mrs. Sheppard,' said Sam

'Hello to you Sam Sheppard,' she said.

They made there way to the bus station and climbed aboard a very modern bus that would take them the 280 miles to Las Vegas, Nevada. They talked about how they would handle the man and wife situation as neither Sam or Fay had ever been married.

'We'll just wing it,' said Sam with a smile.

The coach pulled into the car park of the Golden Nugget 5 hours after leaving Los Angeles, they registered at the desk and retired to there room. Sam collapsed on the bed and Fay dropped in beside him.

'Hows it going so far honey,' she said with a laugh.'

'It's going to be ok kiddo,' said Sam.

They monitored the comings and goings of the four thugs, two shadowed her during the day from 9am till 6pm and then departed for there apartment block just off Westheimer. Then the other two goons took over the watching brief on Katrina until she was ready to quit for the day. As this pattern never changed Sam told Fay he was ready to make a move, so he took a cab to the burger joint just across the freeway from the body-guards residence aand waited. At 3pm he made his move he casually strolled across to there apartment, easily picking the lock and was inside the building within 20 seconds. He settled in the kitchenette checked the beretta with the silencer and was good to go.

At just after 4pm the two goons entered the building one headed to the bedroom the other to the shower. Sam waited for one of the bodyguards to enter the kitchenette and as the guy turned into view Sam let two shots go one to the chest and one to the head, he must have hit the spot as blood cascaded all over the floor, on furniture and on the walls. The guy was dead before he hit the deck, crashing through the furniture and laying very still on the blood soaked floor.

'What was that are you ok Alex?'

The shower then turned off and thug number two ran into the kitchen area to be met by 4 rounds from Sam's 9mm beretta, he joined his buddy on the kitchen floor.

Sam let himself out of the apartment ensuring that the door was securely locked and went across the road to the burger joint and ordered a coffee.

After a ten minute wait Fay drove into the car park entered the burger joint and sat down alongside Sam. Sam signalled the girl behind the counter for another coffee.

'I've been a busy girl while you have been paying a friendly visit to the brother's grim.' she said.'

'I've been working on the explosive device, the timing and the signal to activate it, I think we can go tonight, I reserved dinner at the hotel, she will probably quit around 9pm, that's the norm,' said Fay.

They sat down to dinner at 7.30 and Sam noticed that the limo was parked in it's usual place in a reserved area. He asked to be excused went to the room and collected the device which he transported in a Golden Nugget free carry bag. It was dark in the car park when he placed the magnetic device under the rear wing, he added extra C4 putty, and switch on the device now ready to be activated.

At 8.45 Fay left the table and quietly entered the car park and sat in the hired car. At smack on 9pm Katrina smiling and waving at everybody in the restaurant left moving like a model on a walkway, through the swing doors and into the rear seats of the limo. The limo set off smoothly with the two goons in the front and Katrina draped across the back seat. Fay eased the little hired car into position just behind the limo, wound the window down and pointed the hand held activator towards the rear of the limo and received confirmation that the device had been activated. She signalled to the right and made her way back to the Golden Nugget. She had barely sat down alongside Sam when an enormous explosion rocked the building, causing women to scream and kids running to there parents.

Police sirens and ambulances came flashing by the hotel as the hotel guests assembled outside to see what was going on. A police officer explained that there had been an explosion and it looked like 3 people had died, but it was early days yet and that there are bits of body all over the freeway and the limo has been completely destroyed.

One of the old dears in the party said 'If it's a limo it maybe Miss Katrina, I do hope not she is such a lovely person,'

'Yes she is,' said Sam.

About an hour later a Captain from LVPD called at the hotel and told a restaurant full of people that Ms. Karen Clayton and her two bodyguards were needlessly killed today we think by the Italian Mafia, we are bringing in a few of the mob as we speak,'

The manager then spoke and said,

'Anybody wishing to leave can do so and they will receive there money back, we understand your feelings at this point,' he said.

It was agreed that the whole party would move out in the morning and return to Los Angeles.

CHAPTER 35

Sam and Susan spent a pleasant week-end on the boat and visiting Andrew at his new school. The relationship was developing into something really special, something that neither of them had for many years. After a busy Sunday visiting Andrew and Doctor Jon, they returned to the boat had a couple of martini's and went to bed. The following morning Sam showered, changed and went to his teaching job at Goleta high. After soccer training at 4pm he travelled back to the "Jon Jo" and he noticed that Susan's Pinto was missing from her parking spot. He got on board and dashed to the shower, changed for evening class, he then sat down at his office table to review his mail. He stood up and stretched his legs and noticed a buff coloured letter and a sealed envelope on top of it marked Sam,

He read the buff coloured letter from General Clyde Peterson, it read, Excellent job Sam clean and tidy, I've jumped your retainer up to 50000 dollars. Damn thought Sam why the hell didn't I destroy after reading.

He then opened up the envelope and read: Hello Sam, I was just cleaning up the place and as I was emptying the trash I found this open letter from the Pentagon, I decided to place it on your desk, but the words Las Vegas popped off the page. I have been watching the news on the TV the headlines being the massacre in Vegas, what I didn't know of course was that it was carried out by my closest friend and lover. I have a problem with this Sam, I cannot have any involvement with a killer, the worrying thing for me was you didn't seem to be bothered about it and were carrying on as normal with not a trace of remorse. So Sam our relationship is over, please do not try to make contact with me as it's painful enough as it is. Good bye, Susan.

Sam arrived a little late at evening class to find Susan at her normal desk with the desk to her immediate left where Sam usually sat was empty. Sam went left and found a desk on row 3. After an hour the lecturer said time for a coffee and everybody adjourned to the cafeteria. Sam stayed in his seat and talked with a few of the teacher's surrounding the lecturer.

'We will be discussing on Wednesday how do we help the kids who are falling behind the rest of the class and how to get them up to speed. Goodnight everybody I'll see you on Wednesday'. Sam waited until Susan had left before taking his time reaching his car, Susan was already long gone. The evening class on the Wednesday went as per on with the Monday, with Susan and Sam not making any eye contact.

'We have a big day on Friday with most of the day taken up with lectures on topics that will be included in your first end of term exam, so ladies and Gentlemen listen and learn,'

The following day in the evening Sam was watching a re-run of American Football on the TV when the phone rang.'

'Hello Sam Lassiter,'

'Mr. Lassiter this is Doctor Kramer, I've come to ask a favour, young Andrew has taken a backward step in his development, he doesn't take part in any group studies, he is depressed and sometimes gets violent, he keeps on asking to see you. I'm aware that you and Susan are no longer together but it would be good for you to come over and spend a little time with him.'

'If it's ok with his Mother of course I'll come and see him,' said Sam.

'Susan is so worried about him, she agreed instantly for you to go and see him' said Doctor Kramer.

'Friday 4.30 pm I'll be there Doctor, set it up,' said Sam.

The Friday day session went well and Sam was confident that he would sail through the first term exams. At 4pm Sam made a quick exit and jogged to his car and set off to see Andrew. Andrew was sitting away from his classmates with head bowed concentrating on a puzzle.

'High troublemaker,' said Sam.

Andrew looked up and with a broad smile on his face ran across to Sam and jumped. into his arms.

'I thought you had forgotten about me Sam, you haven't been to see me for ages, and Mum says she has not seen you to talk to,'

'I'll be coming in to see you every Friday about this time if that's ok with you Andrew and if you like some Saturdays and Sundays as well, you do know that I'm a busy man don't you,' said Sam.

'That would be wonderful Sam, I know that you and Mum have split up but if the truth was really known she still loves you as much as I do,' said Andrew.

'So it's back to normal for you my boy, no more tantrums, cut out the violence and back off the depression bouts. Are we clear sir,' said Sam.

'Now that you are going to be coming in to see me, I can do anything and I promise to behave if my illness allows,' said Andrew.

'That's all I can ask Andrew,'

The call came from one of the Nurses that it was time for bed, Andrew said thank you to Sam for coming and said that he would work hard and try to be good, and that he would look forward to next Friday when Sam visited again. He gave Sam a high five and went into his sleeping quarters.

'Thanks for coming over Sam, you can see how pleased he was to see you,' said Doctor Kramer.

'If you have Susan's time with him recorded maybe you can let me know and I can schedule my visits to avoid contact,'

'I'll send you a list Sam,' said the Doctor shaking Sam's hand and thanking him for the visit.

Sam was going to have a quiet week-end studying his class work and preparing next weeks geography and history lessons with 2a and 3a. He also made time in his schedule to go and see the progress of Donna Douglas's girls football team. He then cancelled Susan's and Andrews surprise holiday tickets to the UK in the summer, and rebooked for just himself.

The rest of the term went by in a flash and Sam found himself in the middle of an end of term examination again. It was pretty basic stuff and Sam breezed through it, with plenty of time to check and re-check his work, satisfied he dropped the completed document on the lecturer's table and joined some other early finisher's in the canteen for a coffee.

Susan came in and flopped down at a table close to Sam's group, she gave Sam a quick smile before taking a sip of coffee.

'Going anywhere nice this summer Sam,' said one of the students,

'Yep flying to the UK to see my friends on Monday, I'll be working on my friends estate for a month and then spend a week in Paris, I need to go to my beloved Louvre again,'

'What a wonderful trip, have a good time Sam,' they echoed.

'Nearly perfect only two things missing,' he said as he wandered back into the examination room.

On the Sunday before Sam's departure to Europe Susan was asked to go along and see Doctor Kramer for an update on Andrew.

'We did not want to submit you to any additional stress so I kept a few things from you, I've never done that before but it proved to be the correct way to go,' said the Doctor.

'During the last three months Andrew has had a number of set backs, with depression, loneliness and at one stage violence, he didn't want to see me, the nurse or you Susan, he kept calling for Sam. On three occasions I've called Sam between 2am and 3am and he arrived at the school within a half an hour and within 20 minutes his pulse and blood pressure had returned to normal and he settled down and slept peacefully. This is worrying for me Susan as Sam is off to Europe for 6 weeks holiday.'

'I have prescribed a new drug for Andrew it's called Risperidone which will calm him down and make him less agitated,' said Doctor Kramer.

Doctor Kramer's internal phone bleeped.

'Doctor, Mr. Lassiter is here,'

'Send him in Heather,'

Sam entered the office and shook hands with the doctor and gave a nod and a smile to Susan.

'I think we have done all that we can during your last few visits Sam to try and lesson the blow of you not being available for 6 weeks, Andrew seems to have accepted this, he is not happy about it, but I think he is going to be ok,'

'His profound new interest in Astronomy thanks to you Sam has centered his mind, we have a very clever young man here, he looses me when he talks about the physics, chemistry and meteorology and motion of celestial objects,'

'He has lost me on many occasions Doc,' said Sam.

'If I could go and see him now before he gets to tired, I have a new book for him, he's been asking for it for weeks,' said Sam.

'Lets all go down and see the lad, it will take the heat out of you leaving Sam,' said the doctor.

The four of them spent a lovely hour with Andrew who seemed quite stable and cheerful.

'I'm feeling a little tired Mum I need to rest my eyes from the wonderful book that Sam bought me, and Sam you promised to write to me, I'll see you in 6 weeks,' he said giving Sam a hug and then taking his Mum's hand and heading of to his bedroom.

Sam said his good bye to Doctor Kramer and headed for the car park, he paused and looked up at Andrews bedroom and there he was in the window smiling and waving to Sam. Sam waved back and got into his Dino.

Susan appeared on the passenger side and said.

'I'm so envious of you going over to Europe I've always wanted to go to Paris,' she said.

'I cancelled your ticket and Andrew's ticket 4 weeks ago,' he said with a sad smile on his face.

'See you in 6 weeks, have a good summer holiday,' he said as he roared off in the Ferrari.

CHAPTER 36

Sam hitched a ride with Monique to LAX and boarded the flight to Chicago where he would pick up a direct flight to London Heathrow.

He landed safely at Heathrow and proceeded through immigration and customs without any problems, he stopped at a magazine shop and purchased some postcards, he then went through to the perfume shop and bought three lots of D'or for Lance's wife, Katherine and Trisha. He then boarded a Greenline bus to Camberley. He took a window seat as the bus weaved it's way through crowded traffic and headed south west towards Staines on the A31.

He closed his eyes when the bus took the tight right hand bend where Janet had her accident and kept them shut for a good two minutes, god it still hurt. He would leave some flowers on the spot on his return to Heathrow in 6 weeks time.

He arrived in Camberley at 10pm and took a cab to Sunningdale Manor. He was greeted by the old guy Spencer who ushered him into the lounge to welcomed by Lance.

Spencer announced,

'Colonel Lassiter, sir,'

'Good to see you Sam,' said Lance giving Sam a bear hug.

'Good to see you to buddy,' said Sam.

'Take the Colonels baggage to his usual room please Spencer,'

'Of course sir,' said Spencer.

Sam sat one side of a huge sofa opposite Lance and said,

'You look so much better Lance, I was worried with your harrowed looks the last time I was over,'

'I had huge pressure on me from the bank, the estate was losing money, in fact we nearly had to sell and get out,' said Lance.

'But we have turned it around and are showing a tidy profit, I'll show you around tomorrow, you won't believe what we have done to the place.'

'Excellent job Lance well done buddy,' said Sam.

In the morning prior to the gates being open to "joe" public, Lance gave Sam a tour of the new attractions at Sunningdale Manor and the Estate. There was a playing area for kids with swings, round-a-bouts and slides, riding lessons for beginners, paddle boats on the river, merry-go-rounds, bumper cars, and a steam boat looking like an old Mississippi paddle steamer.

At 10am a large crowd was allowed in, paying there entrance fee to two attractive young ladies stationed at the main gate. They greeted all the visitors with huge smiles and welcomed them to Sunningdale Manor.

Katherine dressed as normal in a white blouse and khaki jodhpurs greeted them both with huge bear hugs, squeezing nearly all the air out of Sam.

'I'm short of staff today Lance, Peggy and Sally are ill,'

'Can I help Kate,' said Sam

'You've got a job Sam,' said Katherine.

Sam spent the rest of the day taking little ones for horse rides while Mummy and Daddy stood nervously by.

He returned to his room knackered, still feeling the effects of jet lag and quietly went to sleep.

The following week he put himself about the estate helping out where necessary in the various activities. In his spare moments he sat in Janet's gallery opposite there favourite Degas when Lance came in and sat along side him.

'Brings back sad memories Sam,'

'Believe it, but some good ones too,' said Sam.

'i'll be taking a week off next week Lance, I'm going to make my last visits to Camberley, Lympstone and Bickleigh, Most of my friends are now retired or have left the Corps, so I have only a few guys to see,' said Sam.

Sam retired to his room and selected a card with a London bus circulating Buckingham Palace and wrote to Andrew.

CHAPTER 37

Sam took the ageing Allard out on the A31 and gunned it all the way to Camberley, checked in at the gate, he was expected. The CO would very much like to meet him at 1400 hours in the Officer's Mess.

Sam entered the Officer's restaurant and asked a young waitress if Mrs. Jeavon's was on duty.

'I'll go see Sir,'

'Colonel Lassiter I heard you were in town, it's good to see you,' she said giving Sam a squeeze.

'I see you are still as ugly as you used to be,' he said.

'Just a few wrinkles Sam, you are looking good it must be that California sunshine,' said Trisha.

'I still think about Trevor a lot and it hurts like hell probably the same as you regarding Janet,' she said.

'There is a potential new guy in my life, he's a little older than me but he really is a nice guy and young Thomas adores him.' said Trisha.

'Talking about Thomas I want a favour from him, I have a little 11 year old friend in Santa Barbara who is autistic and I wondered if Thomas could be his pen pal,'

'I'm sure Thomas would jump at the chance,' she said.

'Why don't you come around to my place at say 7pm and you can see Thomas and I'll introduce you to Fred.' she said.

The evening was really nice It was good to see young Thomas again and to be introduced to Fred who came across as a nice guy, I hoped that Trisha and he could settle down. Thomas loved the idea of a pen pal in America and started writing straight away, he finished a half an hour later, put the letter in an envelope and asked Sam to post it to his new friend.

Sam left the same time as Thomas went to bed and returned to the officers quarters and went to bed. He had agreed with Trisha and Fred to meet the following Saturday at the Annual Sunningdale Summer Ball.

The next few days were spent remembering the good days at Lympstone and Bickleigh and saying goodbye to his remaining friends, this would be the last time Sam would visit the Depots

On the Friday morning he drove back to the Manor, sought out Lance and was guided to the mini steam engine run to act as a porter.

There was a little skuffle in the queue area and Sam went over to find out what was going on, two youths were pushing little children aside and climbing into the open carriages.

Sam went over to the two youths and said,

'There are three ways to go, one get out of the carriage now, two i'll take you to the police station, or three you can both go to intensive care at the local hospital, it's your choice what is it going to be?' said Sam.

The two youths looked at Sam's powerful body and over developed biceps and decided the best way was to leave. He told two security guys to escort the lads to the exit.

On the Saturday night Sam decked out in an Armani suit,lauren shirt, silk tie and italian shoes entered the ballroom and made his way over to Lance's table where Katherine and her latest beau were sitting next to Lance's wife Yvonne along side Trisha and Fred. Sam sat down and joined them.

The Royal Engineer's dance band were brilliant, the food excellent and a good time was had by all.

The next day found Sam repairing a collapsed bridge that spanned the river, he was waist deep in water as he struggled to bolt. the new support brackets in place. He decided to put an extra strut to strengthen the new supports, he was pleased he did this as the safety officer commented on the fact as he produced a safety clearance certificate.

On the Wednesday before the week-end that he was due to fly back to the States, one of the young helpers invited Sam to a skittles evening at the local pub in the village.

'It's only about a half a mile we can walk it if you like,' sha said.

'Fine, I'll be at the main gate at 7,' said Sam.

Sam didn't realise how pretty this young lady was, 5 feet 8 inches tall, long blond hair in a pony tail, toned figure and a pair of massive tits. All she had on was a pair of jeans, a Sunningdale Manor tee shirt and some training shoes.

Sam was coming up to 38 years old now and he must show a little respect for this young lady, "Jesus" she was just eighteen years old.

The evening was good fun with the local village team just edging out the Sunningdale team by 4 pins. Although we all left the pub together it didn't take long for Sam to be alone with Sally making there way slowly back to the Manor, both being a little bit tipsy.

It was a hot balmy August night as they strolled back towards the manor.

'Jesus it's hot,' said Sally slipping her tee shirt over her head to reveal two magnificent breasts with nipples standing out like organ stops and a cleavage to compete with cheddar gorge. Sam took off his tee shirt and pulled Sally close to him and then he lost it, he kissed her and touched her all over and she responded with interest. They made love under the trees completely oblivious to cars that were passing on the manor driveway.

At breakfast the following morning a sheepish Sally and an embarrassed Sam sat together and talked about everything other than there frolic in the bushes.

'I'm sorry for climbing all over you last night, I should know better,' said Sam.

'Forget it Sam, I enjoyed every minute,' she said.

The remaining few days went quickly and before he new it he was being transported to Heathrow by Katherine in the Templeton's Allard. They stopped for a brief moment at the lay-by adjacent to Janet's accident area and places a bunch of red roses. Neither of them spoke they just stood quietly for a short time, Katherine holding hands with Sam.

Sam told Katherine that he would be coming over for Christmas as he said goodbye outside the Departure area.

He spent some time in the Duty Free, bought some wine and cigarettes for Manuel, some perfume for the girls and a cool tie for Doctor Jon. He had a good look in the bookshop and found a "Learners Guide to the Galaxy", which he bought for Andrew.

The flight to Chicago was uneventful and Sam spent most of his time sharing between reading and sleeping.

They touched down at O'Hare and were grounded for an hour before proceeding to LA. It was late evening when Sam boarded the Greyhound for Santa Barbara for the 80 mile trip. At Santa Barbara bus station he took a cab to the marina and by 1am was safely on board and nursing a martini.

Sam had a full week to prepare for the winter term, he consulted the syllabus to ensure he had all the options covered and after four hours completed his work, he continued producing lessons for 1 and 2c, the kids with learning difficulties. Sam was getting more interested in these kids who were having problems and spent hours in the staff room talking with Clare Peacock the leader covering below par students. Clare welcomed Sam's input and was quietly suggesting to Principal Clark that Sam should join her team.

After lunch Sam phoned Doctor Kramer.

'Hi Doc, I'm back, hows our boy Andrew?'

'Hello Sam, the lad is doing very well he is responding to treatment, very few bouts of depression, I'm really pleased with his progress. Which is more than I can say about his mother, she tries to be happy every time she comes into see Andrew, but it's a strained effort, she has lost weight and has to many headaches, i'm a little worried about her Sam,' said Doctor Kramer.

'I have some presents for him from the UK and would like to drop them off, what would be a good time Doc?'

'Anytime after 5pm would be good, Susan and that apology for a man she is with will be long gone by then.'

'Incidently I have banned the boyfriend from meeting Andrew as the lad gets edgy and goes into his shell, he stays in the car park while his mother visits.'

Sam arrived at the boarding school just after 5pm, parked the Ferrari and made his way to Reception where he was directed to the play area where Andrew was as usual his head burried in a book. He looked up and saw Sam and his whole face lifted and with a huge smile ran over to Sam and embraced him.

'Great to see you buddy,' said Sam, as he handed over his present.

Andrew ripped the fancy paper off and was so excited to see the exploded view of Saturn on the book cover.

'I love it, thank you so much Sam,'

The bell sounded which meant that visiting time was over, Sam said his goodbye and told Andrew he would be in to see him after class on Friday.

Friday the day release day came and went, Susan still looking a little sad and not making any eye contact with Sam. She did however take a vigorous stance in the debating group.

The results of the end of summer term examinations were handed out, the majority in the safe area of B or B+, Sam a little better managed an A.

The Michaelmas term plodded on with Sam's teaching duties being extended, with him spending time with 1C and 2C, the classes with kids with learning difficulties. He was under the guidance of Christine Baker who monitored Sam through his first lessons and with her help was developing new methods of getting the message through to these young students.

On the Wednesday evening Sam was in the same group as Susan for a debate on "Punishment or not". It was the first time for a long time that Sam had been in touching distance of Susan. As he sat close to her, memories came flooding back to when they were an item.

At a mid evening coffee break Susan spoke to Sam.

'How are you keeping Sam, how was your trip to Europe,'

'I had a wonderful time at the Manor, trying to help out and working hard. I did manage to get across to Paris for two days, went to the Louvre and the Eiffel Tower.'

Changing the subject Sam said,

'Andy I am told is making wonderful progress, you must be very happy, he is really getting into Astronomy big time,' said Sam'

'Doctor Kramer says he's a natural, good mind and a good learner,'she said\

'Just so that you are aware I visit Andy on a Monday before class and on a Sunday afternoon, he never stops talking about the stars and the universe for the entire 2 hours of my visit.

'They have a Christmas Party next Sunday, I can meet you there if you like,' said Susan.

'Great I'll be there,' said Sam.

'By the by I'm getting Andy a telescope for Christmas it's a Orion 'StarBlast' 4 ASNO, it has an option for a camera which has a timer to enable accurate photography. The camera will cost around 300 dollars and it would be a great addition to the scope,' said Sam.

'Yes I'll get the camera, you had better come with me to purchase the thing I'm bound to get it wrong,' she said.

'Lets do it Saturday Sam,'

'Ok, your place at 2pm,'

The Sunday the day of the party at the special boarding school Sam arrived with Susan who was looking radient and more beautiful than ever dressed in a light coloured trouser suit. Andy's eyes lit up as he saw his mom enter the lounge together with Sam. All tension and stress completely absent. They had a great time playing with the girls and boys together with all the other parents joining in. Drinks were taken and everybody took time out from the game playing and relaxed in the spacious arm chairs.

'What are you doing for Christmas Susan,' said Sam.

'Mum and Dad are flying in from Pheonix and I'm cooking, which I'm not looking forward to doing, I'm a hopeless chef,'

'Got a better idea Susan, why don't you and Andy together with your folks dine with me at Filippo's on Christmas Day, I know he would love to see you and Andy again, it's been a long time, and it would certainly take the pressure off you.'

'You have yourself a deal Sam,' said Susan.

Christmas Eve arrived and at 9pm Sam pulled into Doctor Kramer's car park and proceded on to the Conservatory play area where he assembled the telescope and then wrapped it with festive paper. As he was leaving Susan and her Dad showed up with armfuls of presents for Andrew.

'I'll be here in the morning to see Andy open his presents and then on to Fillippo's for lunch, say 2pm is that good?' said Sam.

'Perfect Sam, see you in the morning,' said Charles Mason, Susan's Dad.

Christmas day at Doctor Kramer's place was hectic to say the least, parents and friends mixing with the children and having a good time. Andrew loved his Telescope and was busy setting up the camera for the nights viewing of the universe. At 1pm the Mason family along with Sam set off to Filippo's for lunch.

The meal was lovely with Filippo's two daughters acting as waitresses. At 4pm it was time to go, Susan and her mother returned to Susan's apartment while grandad Mason, Andrew and Sam went to the Kramer school. The janitor let them in and they completed the setting up of the scope and the camera and got a lock on the "plough" and the north pole star. They checked the weather forecast on the TV and it was stable enough for the janitor to open the sun roof of the conservatory. On completion they departed for Susan's apartment.

They all sat around taking part in general conversation, the main topic being the teacher training course.

'So are you coming over to join us tomorrow Sam,' said Charles.

'I'm off to New York to see my friends for a few days, i'll be back in the saddle in a weeks time raring to go on the teacher training course.'

Sam took his leave and left for the Jon Jo where he would study the recent letter from General Clyde Peterson on the sudden increase in membership of the Ku Klux Klan in the Memphis and Birmingham areas. Also a lot of action by the Klan against the blacks, lynchings, house burnings and a general increase in violence.

'Your brief would be if you take it on Sam, to do a number on them as you did the last time in Georgia. These membership figures have go to be reduced.'

'It's going to be a hard task with many things against you, for example the Police Commissioners in Memphis and Birmingham are in bed with the Klan and are delaying any police involvement for up to an hour after the attacks have been made. A recent burning of a Baptist church in Birmingham where 4 blacks perished, and two Iraqi's were accidently killed being mistaken for blacks. The delay in the police attendance was 30 minutes after the incidents,'

'Do you want to take part in this mission Sam?', call me,'

Sam called right away and accepted the brief, asked for more information on the top Klan members in Georgia and Alabama, then booked his air ticket to Birmingham in one of his diary of names.

CHAPTER 38

Sam checked in at his motel out near the airport and settled down to review additional information from Virginia.

Birmingham, Alabama has been renamed Bombingham. Two civil rights activists members Goodman and Cherry were brutally murdered by the KKK, and the number of beatings was on the increase. The top man in the area for the Klan was Cyrus Clayborne, who was a prosperous wine grower in the area and very out spoken on control of the blacks. Every year Clayborne had his annual bash where he invited all the top men in the Klan from Georgia, Mississippi and Alabama, the occasion was a platform for all the members to vent there feelings regarding the negro's and to drink themselves stupid on this years vintage wine.

Sam took delivery of a package at the motel and went through it in detail. The package contained a lethal mix of barbituates, a paralytic, and a potassium solution, a deadly combination. Two hypodermic needles were in the package with directions on what mix of chemicals was required. A further note from the General saying that he has an agent inside Clayborne's place. She would turn off the burglar alarm at 2am

Saturday for 2 hours which would leave Sam time to poison some of the vintage wine stocked in the cellar.

At 1.45 am on the Saturday, Sam dressed in all black silently drifted into Clayborne's palace, he was confronted by two Rockweiller's who he immediately silenced by throwing some raw steaks in there direction with enough drugs in them to put a rhino out.

He advanced to the back door which had been unlocked by the insider, he entered checked the burglar alarm was off and made his way to the cellar, via the lounge and the kitchen. The cellar was immaculate all the bottles clearly identified in type of wine and dated. Sam got to work with his hyperdermic and contaminated 250 bottles of wine. Only a slight needle point was visable through the cork and the wrapper. Job completed, Sam retraced his steps and out of the rear door, pausing for a moment to ensure that the insider re-locked and re-set the alarm. He passed the two dogs who were gradually coming round, reached the gate and then jogged the 2 miles to his car.

He travelled back to the motel, parked the car outside room 34 and went along to the reception area, he went behind the counter and re-set the CCTV which he had put on hold prior to leaving for Clayborne's place. He went to his room stripped off all his clothes and placed them in a large plastic bag. By 5am he was ready for bed and he slept soundly until 12 noon. He checked out of the motel and drove to Birmingham International Airport where he parked up alongside a lime green Elderado, he transferred the bag with the contaminated clothes and needles into this vehicle. The driver of the Eldorado a Pentagon Agent didn't even speak he just rammed it in gear and was gone.

Sam off-hired the Chevrolet from Hertz, went to another hire service and hired a car under a different name, he made his way to the 1 – 22 which led on to the US 78W and a direct route to Memphis, Tennessee. Two hundred and forty miles later Sam checked in a Motel near the airport to start the time he hated most, the waiting. The shit hit the fan big time at 11pm, Police, FBI, CIA and a whole bunch of Ambulances appeared on the TV news. There was a mass of red, blue and orange lights all assembled in the expansive drive way of Lancaster's huge house. Many body bags were laid out on the front lawn with medics running all over the place. A TV reporter managed an interview with the Police Commissioner, some of his comments went unheard with all the noise that was being generated.

'We have 37 deaths, 10 more in intensive care and not likely to live, the only three not poisoned are all non-drinkers. Yes it's true it was Cyrus Clayborne's annual wine tasting for prominent members of the Klan, the wine had been got at and contaminated with vast sums of poison, we don't know the exact chemicals but whatever it was it was lethal. We at this time do not know who was responsible for these murders, but leaf-lets scattered around the estate point to a middle east operation as opposed to a black power mission.'

Next up in front of the camera's was FBI agent in charge Cole Davenport.

'What's your take on this agent Davenport,' said the reporter,

'Early to say we are looking at letters strewn all over Mi Clayborne's back yard intimating that Jihadist's are not particularly bothered about blacks being violated by the Klan, but the slaying of two young Jihads was a different matter, the letter finished "You don't want to be messing with us, we are not ignorant blacks,' he said.

Sam boarded the red eye at Memphis and slipped into a window seat, closed his eyes and dosed off for the majority of the flight to Los Angeles. He passed through arrivals and customs, went to long term parking picked up the Dino and for the first time in a long time drove the 80 odd miles to Santa Barbara within the speed limits.

CHAPTER 39

He arrived at the boat in the early hours of Monday, showered and went straight to bed, he slept soundly for eight hours. He combed the various TV stations gathering as much information on the Klan massacre as possible. He liked what he heard, the FBI Agent in Charge said that a task force of FBI and US Marshal's has been set in place, there prime task to establish who was responsible for this carnage, we are looking at Black Supremists, black religious leaders and looking closely at local Muslim residents.

'You remember two Jihads were accidentally slain by white activists mistaking them for blacks,' he said.

Sam turned off the TV satisfied that nothing can be traced to him or the Pentagon. He had dealt a severe blow to the KKKs recruitment drive.

He was relaxing in the upper lounge of the Jon Jo when the phone rang.

'Hello Sam, it's Doctor Kramer,'

'Hi Doc, how are you,'

'Some news which you are not going to like Sam, Susan has asked me to call you, she for reasons she is keeping to herself doesn't want you to see Andrew anymore, she would like you to keep away from him, I really don't understand her logic, Andrew's progress during the last few months has been excellent and most of the improvement was down to you, can you tell me what the hells going on Sam,'

'No I can't Doc, but if that is what she wants, so be it, if you could keep me informed on Andy's well being it would be appreciated.'

'Within the patient confidentiality boundary's I'll try Sam.

'Lets see what kind of reaction we get from the lad when he finds out that he won't be seeing you anymore, I'm expecting a bad reaction,' said Doctor Kramer.

Although Sam had cover in place with the air tickets to New York, he was not sure that Susan bought it, this young lady was cute, thought Sam.

For the rest of the week Sam prepared for next terms work at Goleta High and did some reading on what was coming up at teacher training.

He wanted to introduce a new programme for the kids with learning difficulties, he would call it "Great Lives" where he would have visual displays of famous people and take them through there lives from cradle to the grave. He started with a profile of George Washington and then prepared three more Dwight Eisenhower, Winston Churchill and Joe Stalin.

He went into school on the Friday and met up with Donna and Len Partridge the Biology teacher, they all sat down for a coffee and a chat in the staff room. Principal Clark popped her head into the staff room and was invited to sit and have a coffee.

'I've got an idea for 1C and 2C who as you know I take for history, I don't seem to be getting through to the kids so I have an idea to bounce off you,' said Sam.

He went through his "Great Lives" programme with Sharon Clark and she loved it.

'Go for it Sam, I like the visuals,'she said.

The first day back at school went well 2a and 3a refreshed and ready to learn and 1 and 2c loved the life story of George Washington.

Monday's evening class was uneventful Sam taking his position two rows before the front and Susan in her normal seat at the back of the class, not once did she look in the direction of Sam. She also kept well away from Sam at the coffee break. Sam could see that she was struggling but made no effort to engage her in conversation. At the end of the session she gathered her books and made a quick exit. Sam and a few of the student teacher's went to a local bar and had a quiet drink.

The next day Sam was sitting in the Staff Room in the late afternoon when the phone rang, Donna picked it up and said 'Sam it's for you,'

'Hello Sam Lassiter,'

'Sam it's Filippo, I have a very upset young lad sitting in my restaurant, he says he has run away from his school and he wants to see you right now,'

'Tell him to relax and I'll be with him in 20 minutes,'

'Ok, see you soon,' said Filippo.

Sam picked up his bags and sprinted to his car, roared it into life and set off for the Marina.

'What the devil have you been up to, your Mum and Doctor Kramer must have worried themselves to bits,' said Sam.

'They won't let me see you Sam, but I told them if they won't let me see you I would run away,' said Andy.

'Ok settle down now Andy, lets sort this out,' said Sam.

Sam phoned Doctor Kramer and explained that Andrew was with him on the boat and he could pick him up when he wished.

When Doctor Kramer and Susan arrived at the Jon Jo, Andrew was already fast asleep on the huge sofa in the upper lounge.

'You know he smashed his telescope and threw the camera across the play area,' said Susan,

'I didn't know that, he didn't say to much between the tears,' said Sam.

'So it's your call Susan, it's obvious the lads condition has deteriorated since the exclusion of Sam,' said Doctor Kramer.

'Are you prepared to come and visit Andy again Sam, say once a week on a Sunday,' said Susan.

'If you are sure you are ok with that, yes of course it would be great to see my little friend on a regular basis,'

'Now what about tonight ae you going to take Andy back to his room at the school, or let him stay over. If you both want to stay on board tonight there is plenty of room,' said Sam.

'I think it would be a good idea for Andy to stay here tonight with you Sam, and Susan if you could also stay it would be good for the lad to wake up and see both of you, I however have to attend a charity bash tonight and would have problems with Mrs. Kramer if I missed it,' said Doctor Kramer.

'I'll stay Sam,'

'I'll order some food from Filippo's, get you some sleeping gear and we are sorted,' said Sam.

Susan placed her hand on Andy's shoulder and closed her eyes.

'You know Sam I was scared to death when he escaped from the school, he could have been abducted, he could have been involved in a traffic accident, all things crossed my mind,'

'He's safe now Susan,' said Sam as he crossed the lounge to his desk and started wading through his "Great Lives" programme for 1 and 2c.

After an hour and a huge portion of lasagne Susan dropped off on the sofa, Sam fetched a pillow and covered her with a smooth blanket.

Sam was an early riser, he took a shower, shaved and dressed in a T and jeans. He went to the galley and prepared breakfast for Susan and Andy who were just stirring.

'I know I'm only supposed to be calling in on Andy on Sundays but I think I had better take a look at the damaged telescope and camera and see if it is not completely totalled,' said Sam.

Susan took Andy back to the school and settled him in, Sam took a look at the scope and decided that he could repair it, the camera however was a total write off with the lenses smashed.

Sam left the school and returned to the marina where he set about repairing the telescope, it required only a few new parts which Sam purchased and fitted. That night on the forward deck Sam zeroed the scope on to the Plough and the North Star, perfect thank god for that he thought.

Sam returned the telescope to the school conservatory early in the morning before the majority of the staff arrived and set it up.

The next few days he retuned letters to the UK and prepared some more "Great Lives" papers.

The Sunday afternoon visitation went well and Andy seemed to have settled into some kind of good rhythm, blood pressure good, and no trace of a tantrum or any feelings of depression.

At 5pm Sam said his goodbye to Andy and after a huge hug departed.

CHAPTER 40

The first Monday of the new term was great, 2a and 3a classes were brilliant and the interest in 1c for the life and times of Florence Nightingale went like a dream. He would talk with Len Sharp the top man on teaching the slow learners to find out if any improvement was being made with the introduction of "Great Lives".

Sam arrived early for Monday evening night classes and made his way over to the desk alongside that usually used by Susan. She came in with a bunch of other students gave them a wave and sat down next to Sam, giving him a little smile. She looked more relaxed tonight, more like the old times, with her make up and her hair perfect, she in fact looked like a million dollars, thought Sam.

The evening class was opened up by the lecturer when he asked each student in turn if they had any ideas on getting through to children with learning difficulties.

Susan's contribution was accepted warmly when she suggested a more love and affection approach, she continued by saying that a lot of these kids do not have a happy home life.

Sam's input was based on his personal method of getting to the kids, his introduction of more visual aids has certainly been a benefit to his pupils in the C streams.

The Wednesday evening class came and went as per normal, just an interesting evening. On the Friday day release, plenty of work and discussion on exploring in depth teaching and learning.

Sam left immediately at the finishing time of 4pm and returned to his boat, he sat down and reviewed his programme for the oncoming week. At 9.30pm his phone rang waking him up from a little power nap.

'Hello,' said Sam,

'Hello yourself this is Sergeant Desi Carpenter reporting for duty,'

'Des, lovely to here from you how are you,'

'I'm good, I have a few days off before I fly off to Mexico to film a new western, I was hoping to come and see you and maybe you can run over a few lines of dialogue with me,'

'You have open boat here Des, what's your ETA,'

'I'll get the studio chopper up to you in the morning say 11am, looking forward to seeing you.' She said her goodbye's and put the phone down.

Sam was out on deck in the morning with his binoculars trained towards the south trying to seek out Desi's helicopter. He located a little dot in the distance hugging the south California coastline and speeding it's way northwards, as it approached the Santa Barbara marina helipad it circled an gently landed slap bang in the middle of the pad. Two beautiful long brown legs emerged from the chopper followed by the exquisite Desiree de Carlo.

She trotted off the landing ramp pulling her little case behind her, and fell straight into the arms of the waiting Sam, they stayed locked together for what seemed a lifetime. Sam took her little case and they went on board.

'Lets get to work on that script of yours,' said Sam.

So three martini's later they were well into the swing of the new script. Des was having problems with a few lines of Spanish in the script.

'Not to worry my cleaning lady will be in later she can help with the pronunciation,' said Sam.

'I've washed the mosquito net and stored up on the antiseptic cream so you should get a trouble free sleep,' said Sam jokingly,'

'Maybe I don't want a trouble free sleep Sam, maybe I want you to trouble me,' she said with that cheeky smile on her face.

'Ok lets get this screen text sorted, I want you word perfect before you leave,' said Sam.

'Yes coach,' she replied.

They went through the whole dialogue twice and apart from the few words of Spanish Desi was in good shape.

'I need to phone Monique,' said Desi

'Go for it,' said Sam.

'Hi Monique, it's Desi de Carlo, I'm staying on Sam's boat for a couple of days and would love to see you,'

'I have a very tight schedule at the moment Desi and today's the only space I have,'

'Lets do lunch and then go shopping, what do you say?'

'I say yes, I'll be over in 20 minutes,' said Monique.

I'll see you guys later, don't spend to much money,' said Sam with a laugh waving them off.

Sam settled down to write some letters to the UK, took 5 minutes out to reserve a table at Filippo's. When his correspondence was completed at around 6pm he took a shower, shaved and dressed in a white Polo shirt,

Giorgio Armani trousers and Italian shoes. Desi arrived with armloads of packages, Sam noticed that they were all designer labels.

'It looks like you had a good time,'

'We both did, it was lovely to see her again,' said Desi.

'We dine in two hours Des, so do you remember where the showers are?'

'I'm on my way,' she said.

Desi appeared back in the lounge at 7.30 looking like a million dollars, she was wearing a Mary Quant black mini dress with two thin supporting straps, a black choker with a diamond in it, no stockings or tights and a pair of black high heeled designer shoes. She looked every inch a movie star as they both walked the short distance across the quay side to Filippo's.

They were greeted by the man himself, who showed them to a corner table overlooking the marina. Filippo had a 4 piece band in place all excellent musicians with a sound reminiscent of the great George Shearing.

A little girl coyly approached Desi and asked for an autograph. Desi reached into a carrier bag that she had brought with her and pulled out some photo's of herself.

'What's your name honey,' she said,

'It's Allison, Miss de Carlo,' she said politely.

The little girl was beside herself as she returned to her parents, excitedly showing proudly the photo of Desi. This started an avalanche of autograph hunters, Desi didn't seem unduly stressed with this and duly signed away for a half an hour. Things settled down and Desi and Sam were aloud to enjoy there meal. In between the starter and the main course and between the main course and the desert Sam and Desi had slow romantic dances.

'Every time I get anywhere close to you I rise to the occasion, you will have to stay close to me when we return to our table or people will get a view of the crown jewels,' joked Sam.

'It's nice to know I can still make it work,' said Desi.

As they both sat down Desi looked across to Sam and said,

'So hows your love life Sam, I can't believe a handsome son of a gun like you is flying solo,'

'You remember Janet, well when I enrolled for teacher training I couldn't believe what I was seeing, there she was standing in line looking like Janet's twin, her name is Susan . It was instant chemistry and I thought at last I have found someone who I can spend the rest of my life with. Everything was going just fine she introduced me to her 10 year old son Andrew who suffers from autism and was causing her a lot of stress. The kid took an instant shine to me and me to him, he was a nice lad. Then a couple of evenings after returning from Las Vegas I found a crumpled letter alongside the paper garbage bin. It was a letter from my boss at the Pentagon congratulating me on a successful mission in Vegas, she put two and two together and made four.' Looking at the news reel on TV and the carnage at Vegas, she asked me not to see her anymore and please keep away from my son, she said that she couldn't have an association with a violent man.

'So that was that until young Andy threw a violent tantrum, slipped into depression mode, smashed his telescope and camera and ran away from the special school. He ended up waiting for me on board the Jon Jo,'

I phoned the Doctor who collected Susan and came to the marina. They were greeted by Sam who informed them that Andrew had settled down and was asleep in the top deck lounge.

'Susan agreed that I should start seeing Andrew again, and that Sunday afternoon would be a good time, if I was ok with that,'

'So, Andy is on the mend and my relationship with Susan is strained but at least she's talking to me again,'

'Ok that's me done, what about your love life Des, if the magazines and paper's are to be believed you must be having a hell of a time,' said Sam.

'I have never been to bed with any of my leading men or any other member of the crew, where they get the crap they print god only knows,' said Desi.

'When they really go over the top. Sue them for millions Des,'

The rest of the evening was wonderful to feel the closeness of a woman's body again was great thought Sam.

'Thank you for a great night Sam, now all you have to do is make love to me all night,'

'I'm no coward Des, I'll give it a go,' said Sam.

Before they reached the sleeping quarters on the Jon Jo, Sam made his move as they entered the top deck lounge, in one swift movement he unzipped her dress flicked off the shoulder straps causing the dress to fall to the floor. She stood there tall, elegant and beautiful and apart from a black thong completely naked. Sam took off his shirt and trousers and they kissed passionately, before falling in a heap on to the nine seater sofa. They made love only four times that night, it was the quality not the quantity and they were both completely satisfied with there efforts.

Sam was first to rise in the morning and prepared breakfast and as he poured out the orange juice he said,

'I'm going over to see Andy this afternoon, do you want to come with me or rest up?'

'I would love to come with you and meet young Andrew,' said Desi.

They arrived and parked up the Ferrari in the visitors area and signed in at reception. When Andy saw Sam he rushed over and gave him a huge bear hug.

'Andy, I want you to meet Desi a good friend of mine,'

'Andrew it's nice to meet you, Sam has told me so much about you,' said Desi.

'Come with me Desi,' he said grabbing her hand and moving in the general direction of his telescope.

'I've set it up to view the Milky Way tonight, but I can't take any pictures because my camera is broken,' he said

'That's a shame, how did you manage to break it,' asked Desi,

'I lost my temper when I had an attack and I threw it and managed to smash the lenses, I acted like a spoilt child, I hope I won't do it again,' said Andy.

'What was the model of the camera Andy,'

'Don't know the model number but I think it was a Voiglander made in Germany,'

The afternoon was great, it was good to see Andy more or less back to normal, he introduced all his friends to Desi who just by being there was the star attraction. Susan arrived as tea was being taken and did a double take on Desi who was being photographed by all in sundry. Desi made her way across the room and introduced herself to Susan.

'Hello Susan, my names Desi, I've heard so much about you from Sam. He's right you are a beautiful girl and should be in the movies,'

'Sam sometimes exaggerates Desi,'

'Completely the opposite Susan, he just calls it as he sees it,

'We will always be close but I'm not sure of anything beyond that,' said Susan.

The end of visiting time bell sounded and everybody made there way out of the building, Desi gave Andy and Susan a hug and joined Sam who walked her to the car park. They drove back in silence to the boat, Sam prepared a tuna salad and they sat down and watched some TV. At midnight they went to bed, no sex but the hug of all hugs before they went to sleep. In the morning Sam woke to find Desi missing, he went into the lounge and found a note left by Des. Gone shopping won't be long. Love Des. . .

She returned an hour later with a nicely decorative package, on the outside it read to my friend Andy from Desi.

'When you see Andy next give him the package please Sam,' said Desi.

The studio helicopter arrived and Desi was gone, waving goodbye to Sam who was standing on the upper deck.

On the Monday Sam had a free morning, his first lesson was 2pm, 1c for one of his "Great Lives" presentations. So in the couple of hours he had to spare he drove out to Doctor Kramers place and left the present for Andy.

'Ok 1c today we are going to talk about President Abraham Lincoln,' said Sam.

The class really enjoyed the lesson, and Sam moved on to give the exact same lesson 1 hour later to 2c.

The Christmas term passed at a steady pace and gradually wound down. All the teacher's passed on there holiday good wishes and left for home. Sam made some long distance phone calls to the UK and wished Lance and family, Katherine, Trisha and Len a merry Christmas. Sam settled in and resigned himself to a quiet Christmas, hoping that the Pentagon didn't need his services.

CHAPTER 41

The Pentagon however did need his services and the following morning a registered letter arrived from Virginia.

Hello Sam,

I'm putting together a team to remove some paedophiles from the face of the earth, I have two agents in San Paulo, and two agents on Bay Shore, Long Island and I need you to team up with Senior Agent in Charge Charlie Gardener in New York.

This is the story, thousands of kids are running wild in San Paulo, Brazil and easy pickings to be abducted, these kids are promised a good life in the USA, the truth is somewhat different. These kids are taken off the streets of San Paulo and then on to the Port of Santos 50 miles due east. They are then shoved into containers with no washing facilities and only one toilet between 40 of them. They are then shipped to Long Island and landed at a remote Bay Shore. We believe these kids are used for the purpose of child porn, prostitution and for Paedophile groups. Our information once the kids get to New York is very limited, I want you to hook up with Charlie and destroy this evil practice. I have arranged for Agent Gardiner to meet you a week today at your address on 5th Avenue. I have also slipped in air tickets from Santa Barbara to New York, via Los Angeles.

Sam completed the final two evening classes and the final day release prior to the Christmas holiday. He told Susan that he would be going to the Christmas party at Andy's school tomorrow, Saturday.

Parents, Doctors, friends and Nurses turned out at the school get together, all the young girls and boys having a wonderful time showing off there presents. Andy had already written to Desi thanking her for the top of the range camera.

'After what I did, I don't deserve friends like you and Desi,' said Andy.

'I think she did her research Sam, this camera is the top of the range, she really is a lovely lady,' said Andy.

'She is about the nicest you are likely to get young Andy, now look after it, treat it like gold dust,'

'I will Sam.'

Susan and Andy were deep in conversation as Sam approached them.

'You two have a wonderful holiday and I'll see you mid January, I'm spending Christmas in New York with friends,' said Sam.

'I'll miss you,' said Andy.

'So will I,' said Susan.

Sam smiled and gave them both a hug and left. . .

The flight to New York was uneventful, Sam spent most of the flight time studying the information supplied by the Pentagon. He had arranged to meet Charlie Gardener in the morning at the Penthouse on 5th Avenue. At exactly 10am the next morning Charlie turned up and to Sam's surprise was a young lady.

'Sorry to look so surprised I expected a guy named Charlie to show up,' said Sam

'Not a problem, it's not the first time Sam,' she said.

'Ok Sam, the kids have left San Paulo and are well on there way to the docking area at Bay Shore, Long Island, I want to be in position waiting for them to disembark. My plan if you agree is to plant tracking devices on the vehicles, this will lead us to the people who supply these sick bastards,'

'I like it, just for the record Charlie hows your skuba swimming and diving?'

'Class A grade,' said Charlie,

'After the crew have taken out the abduction gang in San Paulo, I would like to sink the trawler that brought the kids to Long Island, I'll need 4 standard Limpet mines, skuba gear, and oxygen bottles,'

'I'll sort it,' said Charlie.

Agent Gardener and Sam sat in separate cars and waited for the trawler from Brazil to drop anchor 400 yards from the dockside at,' Bay Shore. Sam slipped into the water and made his way towards the trawler, he dived and placed the four limpets evenly along the hull, set the timer on max and returned to his car. While he was away planting the explosive devices Charlie Gardener was busy placing trackers under the pick up vehicles that had just turned up. Two speed boats appeared from nowhere and collected the kids from the trawler and transferred them onto the waiting vehicles. They pulled out immediately together making there way in the general direction of Manhattan. The trawler made steam, pulled anchor and slowly eased herself into the cold Atlantic ocean heading south.

When the vehicles reached the outer limits of New York they split, so Charlie followed one vehicle and Sam the other.

'We meet up later at my place,' said Sam

'Roger that,' said Charlie.

The two vehicles reached there destinations and one of them offloaded the young children into an Escort Agency in the south of Albany up state New York, the other bus carrying the other boys stopped a further 20 miles north of Albany and unloaded the boys.

Having established the whereabouts of the rent boys, Sam and Charlie met up at the 5th Avenue penthouse.

'I need to get into these Agencies and put some phone taps in place,' said Sam,

'Not a problem Sam, I'll get the NYPD experts on to it as we speak,' said Charlie.

'I want to run this mission alongside the NYPD guys, I'll call the shots and they can execute the take down,' she said.

Now the waiting starts thought Sam as he sat with Charlie in the dirty old pick up van waiting for any calls from punters for the services of rent boys. After sitting in silence for 8 hours the red light started flashing.

'I require your Escort services young lady,' said a man with a well educated voice.

'That's what we are here for sir,' she replied.

I will call you back at midnight tonight, if you want to do some excellent business make sure somebody in authority is there to take our requirements,' the voice said as it curtailed the call.

'I'll be listening too you bastard,' said Sam.

Midnight right on the money the call came through.

'I want 6 rent boys for a secret party at my place, you have no need to know where that is, I will pay and transport the boys to and from my place,' said the caller.

'Very good sir, the costs are as follows and payable up front,' said a director of the Agency.

'You will transport the boys to and from your residence, which we have know interest in where the location is, the boys will cost $2000 each for sex, any deviations, sex games are extra,' he said.

'I will transfer $10000 to your account now, with an extra $5000 for one individual to carry out some sex games, have we a deal?' said the educated voice.

'As soon as the money arrives you can collect the boys sir,'

The next day at 4pm a Limo turned up at the Agency and a guy in uniform handed a package to the Agency director which contained $17000. The boys looking very presentable were then paraded out and loaded into the limo.

The limo eased into the flowing traffic with Sam and Charlie following about four cars behind, hidden by a large heavy duty truck. Twenty minutes later the limo pulled into a fancy tree lined drive which led to a splendid large country house, the limo drove around the rear of the building and set the boys down in the servants quarters.

Sam and Charlie set themselves up in a heavily wooded area 300 yards from the entrance to the house. It was established that it belonged to Senator Simon Lancaster. The guests gradually turned up and Charlie recognised every one of them, one Judge Thomas Singleton, two Para legals from Manhattan, Kyle and Stringer, Carl Mariner from the Juvenile Crime Unit and Captain John Pointer from NYPD in Queens.

'What a collection, I'm going to nail there asses,' said Charlie.

Inside the luxury house the Paedophiles each paired off with a rent boy, the elder 14 year old lad was reserved for Senator Lancaster. So the stage was set, the five guests were seated with there rent boys in the main hall of the house, super eight camera on a tripod in position with one of the footmen filming. The young lad arrived completely naked and set himself down on all fours waiting for the arrival of Lancaster.

As Lancaster appeared the guests and the rent boys cheered and applauded, Lancaster waved to all of them and took off his cloak, he was completely naked bent over the youngster and penetrated his rectum and at the same time put both hands on the kids throat and started to squeeze. As the intensity of the act grew he thrusted harder causing pain to the youngster, his grip getting stronger and stronger on his throat. By the time he had climaxed his grip was white knuckled, in fact to strong, the lads neck and shoulders collapsed and he fell into a heap on the marble floor dead.

Senator Simon Lancaster raised his arms in triumph and then bowed before his guests who yelled in delight "Bravo Bravo".

Lancaster summoned two off his man servants.

'Get this out of here,' he said pointing to the dead youngsters body.

The NYPD Task force was now in position and Charlie gave the word for them to attack, so armed with Glock 17s and a battering ram they advanced on the country house. The ram completely smashed the front door down and 15 officers charged into the room arresting everyone, the paedophiles were handcuffed and read there rights and taken away to a lock up in Albany NYPD. The forensic and crime scene people then moved in gathering all information and secured the snuff movie of the young man.

'We've got the bastards, it's a slam dunk,' said Charlie Gardener.

They both went back to the Penthouse on 5th to complete there reports, Charlie to the FBI and Albany NYPD and Sam to the Pentagon.

'You look so sad Sam, what's the problem,' said Charlie,

'I should have told you to take action before you did and maybe we could have saved the kids life, damn it,' said Sam.

'I'll have to live with that Sam, it was my call,'

'Good luck with the case Charlie make sure the bastards get murder one, and pay a visit to the hot seat,' said Sam as he saw Charlie off, he returned to the Penthouse on 5th Avenue.

CHAPTER 42

Early the next morning a sad and angry Sam boarded the cross town metro to the Bronx, he cursed at his timing on the Albany case, three minutes earlier and he would have saved the life of a young man. He called in at the newly opened Starbucks coffee house and collected one black, one white and one latte, he then picked up three bagel's from a nearby bakery. He weaved his way through the Crown Victoria's jockying for parking spaces and entered the dirty Precinct building. As he passed through the centre of the precinct he heard the microphone switch on.

'No aggravation or violence please from the visiting "Limey",' said the desk Sergeant.

'Morning Mac, are the ladies in the same office as before,'

'Yep Sam, same door, same desk,'

Sam pushed through the door and placed the three coffees on Sergeant Lacey's desk, they both looked up and with huge smiles greeted Sam with a three way hug.

Sam explained his involvement with the NYPD and FBI on the recent Paedophile mission, both girls said that they had read the brief and were so pleased that the perps were now safely locked away.

'We have some news too Sam, we have both received a promotion, me to Lieutenant and my partner here to Detective Sergeant and we have been transferred across to old unsolved crimes,'

'Anytime you need any profiling drop me a line and I'll see what I can do,' said Sam.

After they talked about family and friends, Sam decided it was time to leave for La Guardia and his flight home to Santa Barbara. On the way to the airport he stopped at a book store and purchased "The Sky at Night" by Patrick Moore for a present for Andrew.

The flight home via Chicago was uneventful and Sam spent most of the time catching up on some sleep. It was late evening when Sam finally climbed into his car and started out on the journey north to Santa Barbara.

He sat down and relaxed and prepared some "Great Lives" for the oncoming term. He researched Winston Churchill, Joe Stalin, Florence Nightingale, and some famous French Impressionists, Manet, Monet, Degas, and Cezanne . He then completed his correspondence to the UK and prepared his geography and history pro-grammes for the Easter term.

CHAPTER 43

The next day he visited Andrew, made sure it was after 4pm and gave him his present, he immediately burried his head in the book. While Andrew was busy setting up his telescope for the nights shoot, Sam asked how he was feeling and how his lessons were going.

'I'm in good shape Sam, not to many depression bouts, I think the Doctor has landed on the right meds for me,'

'That's great news Andy,'said Sam,

Just as Sam was preparing to leave Susan showed up sporting a pair of wrap around sun glasses.

'Hi darling,' she said to Andrew.

'What's wrong with your eyes Mom,'

'I have a nasty infection, a sty or something Andrew,'

Sam moved over to the coffee machine and asked if she wanted a drink,

'White would be nice, thanks Sam,'

'You are a terrible liar Susan, how did you get that shiner,' said Sam.

'I parted company with my latest boyfriend and he didn't like it, so he took a swing at me,'

'Would you like me to pop along and pay him a visit and suggest that men do not hit women,'

'God no, I'm not to keen on the guy but I don't want him to end up in intensive care.'said Susan.

'Just a thought,' said Sam.

Sam said his goodbyes to them both and said that he would see Susan at the Monday evening class.

'I would like you to come and sit next to me,' she said.

'That's a deal,'said Sam as he left.

Sam completed his preparation for the Easter term and settled in for a quiet peaceful week-end.

He encountered Principal Clark in the main corridor and she said,

'Sam I have three Graduate Teacher's in house for this term and I would like them to attend one of your "Great Lives" lessons, have you any objections to that,'

'Not at all, they may think my teaching technique is rather unusual but hey, what the heck,' said Sam.

Sam surveyed the 30 students of 1C, together with the Graduate Teacher's and said.

'One year ago you guys were paraded as slow learners and placed in the C stream, your first assessment at that time was D-, your assessment as of now is B+, I have never been so proud of any class of students in my entire life, you have excelled yourselves, well done.' The three graduates stood up and applauded 1C, and called for the whole class o applaud.

'For the first time ever we have an A student, take a bow Marion Miller,' said Sam,

A shy little eleven year old girl stood to a round of applause.

'Now Marion I want you to introduce today's great lives,'

'Today's great lives is Sir Winston Churchill,' she said.

Sam placed a picture of Winston Churchill on the blackboard.

'So who have we got today class,' said Sam.

'Sir Winston Churchill sir,' they all chorust.

Sam took 2C and 3C through the same portfolio of Winston Churchill. At 4pm he changed into his running gear and went to the new 6 lane track surrounding the football field, the floodlights were activated and Sam was pounding the track. The new track and floodlights were a gift from the Santa Barbara local government. He passed the lone figure of Principal Clark who was jogging at a sensible pace. Sam backed of the pace and ran the last few laps with Sharon Clark. When Sam finished his three miler he went straight to the Ferrari and drove home to prepare for college.

It was nice to be back at the college and seeing old friends again, there was a general hustle and bustle in the room as they all related there holiday experiences. Sam sat next to Susan and he could see that she was pleased about that.

'Do you fancy a drink after class,' Sam offered,

'I'd like that Sam, just like old times,' she said.

They sat at a window seat in the "Flamingo" bar in Santa Barbara.

'Hows the eye Susan,'

'More or less ok thanks, I'll lose the shades tomorrow, by the by the guy that did this is on his way back to his wife in Miami, I didn't even know he was married, I must be some kind of idiot,'

'Sometimes in life we do daft things, you are not on your own Susan,'

I'm aware that when we finished seeing each other, and although you didn't show it I think I was very cruel thing for me to do,' she said,

'You did what you thought was right at the time and if I thought deeply about it, I understood where you were coming from, I wouldn't want to go out with me either,' said Sam.

Susan leaned over and planted a kiss on Sam's lips.

'I want you as part of my life again Sam,'

'You of course know that I have never stopped loving you,' said Sam.

For the rest of the evening the two of them were inseparable.

'We must rehearse our presentations to the class, it seems that we both have a lot of work to do, why don't you come over to the boat for the week-end and we can make a start,'

'Great I'll pop in and see Andrew to make sure he is ok and be over to your place say 10pm Friday,'

'Sounds fine to me,' said Sam.

They had a long lingering kiss in the restaurant car park before wending there way home through the evening traffic.

Susan arrived just after 10 and plonked herself down on the huge sofa in Sam's upper lounge,

'We have just one week to get to grips with our presentations, so lets get at it,' said Sam,

'I'm going to put out a "Great Lives" presentation, aimed at kids who have learning difficulties, I was thinking Theodore Roosevelt, and I was hoping that it would be with 1c. They are the kids that really want to learn, a captive audience,' said Sam,

'I have an idea to go more in depth with the elite students in 4a, into the British Industrial Revolution,' said Susan.

They both worked hard on there presentations for the whole week-end, finally reviewing all there notes prior to a full rehearsal the following Wednesday.

Sam kissed Susan on the top of her head and said goodnight as he wandered slowly towards his sleeping cabin. He stripped to a pair of shorts and dozed off. Ten minutes later Susan slid into his bed, she was completely naked, she wrapped her arms around Sam and they went to sleep exhausted.

An agreement was reached between the Santa Barbara Teacher's College and the three major High Schools in the area for teaching students to conduct face to face lessons. These presentations would be closely monitored by the Senior Lecturer's. Sam and Susan were to report to St. Mary's High School on the outskirts of Santa Barbara, Sam to teach 1c. and Susan to teach 3a. Molly Seymour a quiet pretty young lady who sat just in front of Susan was awarded Sam's 1c, at Goleta High.

It was the day release Friday that the locations and timings were posted on the notice board and during the lunch break Molly sought out Sam for some insider information.

'Just remember one thing Molly, my kids in 1c are as bright as buttons and will listen on every word that comes out of your mouth, they are determined to continue the wonderful progress they have made this passed year, going from a class average of 'c-', to a class average 'b.'

'The biggest mistake I made was thinking these kids had learning difficulties, given the right direction these guys can be A students.' said Sam.

'The majority of children at first year who are placed in 'c' streams think that they are losers, it's up to there teacher's to rid them of this theory.'

'I think Netty Singleton who teaches 1c at St. Mary's has the same philosophy as me, as she is making superb progress with these so called learning difficulties students,'

'Thanks for the information Sam, I'll make sure I dot the I's and cross the 'T' in my research,' she said.

'Make sure you involve them during your lesson and you will have great success,' said Sam.

Sam and Susan spent the whole week-end finalising there presentations, both were happy with the final brief. On Sunday afternoon they popped in to see Andrew at the Kramer school, he was in a great mood showing off his most recent coloured photo's of the stars. They were neatly positioned in a album with the Latin name alongside the English name under the photograph.

They said there goodbye's to Andrew and a few of his friends and headed back to the "Jon Jo" and settled down to a nice Lasagne and a really dry martini.

CHAPTER 44

The Wednesday of the hands on teaching arrived and the three adjudicators took there places at the rear of class 1C at St. Mary's as the pupils made there way to there seats.

'Good Morning everybody, my name is Mr. Lassiter and I will be taking you through today's history lesson.'

'A programme we have recently introduced at my other school has proved to be very successful, we call it "Great lives", where we look closely at certain individuals who have contributed to world history,'

'Today's great is Franklin D. Roosevelt, the only American President to be elected four times, I'll take you through his life from 30th January, 1882, until his death in 1945.'

Sam placed a picture of the wheel chaired President on the blackboard, and proceeded to go into detail of the famous man's life.

The lesson went like a dream the whole class apart from one really getting into it. One lad seemed to be staring into space and seemed more interested in what was going on outside in the school grounds than on what Sam was saying.

'Mr. McDonald I can see that you are not with us, you have two ways to go, one, knuckle down and listen with the rest of the class, or two, take a hike to the Principals office, it's your call young man,' said Sam.

'I'll stay and pay attention,'

'You'll stay and pay attention what?' said Sam

'I'll pay attention, sir,' said Stephen McDonald.

'That's good and I'll tell you why young man, when the lesson is over we have a 15 minute question and answers session and you will assist me along with Cathy Springfield.'

The talk on Franklin D ended and Sam ushered up to the front of the class Stephen and Cathy.

'Ok it's question time, direct your questions to me and between us we'll give you an answer.'

The questions came thick and fast, Sam ensuring the the easier ones were answered by the two pupils

The bell sounded the end of the lesson, and Sam thanked both of the kids that helped him through question time. As they returned to there seats they were greeted by a round of applause,

Sam thanked 1C for there attention and wished them luck for the remainder of the term.

He returned to the staff room and analysed his mornings work, making sure that he didn't make the same mistakes the next time.

Two of the three adjudicators came over to him and congratulated him on his presentation. Sam spotted Susan in the corner of the staff room deep into concentration for the afternoons presentation. He wished her good luck and left for the marina for a rest and a very dry martini.

CHAPTER 45

Sam took control of the under twelve's soccer training at 4pm and then stayed on to watch Donna and the girls session at 6pm. After satisfying himself that the soccer programme was progressing nicely Sam returned to the marina and settled in for the evening. He sorted his mail for the UK writing to Lance and Trisha informing them that he would be over during the summer break, and needed assurance from Lance that his grass cutter had been serviced.

The spring term at Goleta High went slowly, but Sam enjoyed the stressless daily routine, and the comradery of the teacher's.

The evening classes and the day release went as planned with Sam recording straight A's in the end of term examinations.

Nothing out of the ordinary happened for the entire summer term, everything progressing nicely, his relationship with Susan was satisfactory but not as it used to be. She still had a problem handling Sam's part time employment as a trouble shooter. Sam believed it was only to ensure that her son stayed on the straight and narrow that she remained friends. Sam accepted this and satisfied himself that the relationship wouldn't go any further. The final day release day at the college was a very relaxing day, with not to much work going on, a sort of party atmosphere in the air.

Sam turned to Susan and said,

'I'm going over to the UK this summer for 4 weeks, would you and Andy like to come with me,'

'I'll clear it with Doctor Kramer regarding Andy's med's and if ok we would love to come with you,'

'I'll await the all clear and then book the tickets for the second week in August,' said Sam.

The last week in July Sam received a letter from Virginia, it read:

The FBI are having problems up in north east Nebraska in a place called Lincoln, we have been asked by the FBI for assistance and you in particular, having experienced your previous work in dealing with the Neo Nazi people. The Kruger family of eight brothers and two sisters are engaged in hard line Nazi business and in the last 3 months the Bureau has lost five agents trying to get these party members to the courts. Also seven young black youths have disappeared, we believe in so called "Nigger Hunts", where the young black guy is offered $500 not to be captured by the hunting party of a dozen armed men. The FBI has an insider at the Kruger farm on contract hire as a combine driver during the current harvest period, she has formed a friendship with the leader of the family, a guy called Seth. A young FBI recruit has volunteered to participate as a runner and we have placed him in a job at the local store, it didn't take long for contact with the Nazi's to take place and he was scheduled to run. Information coming out is that a hunt is due Sunday week, I want you to go to the Kruger farm area and bring them down. Liaise with the Kansas City FBI who will provide back up. I have enclosed a return air ticket to Kansas City, you will collect a Range Rover at the airport and drive to Lincoln where you are booked into the same hotel as Agent Sally Powers. Your cover for this mission is of a phogra-pher setting out pictures for a calender to promote holi-days in the area. Your name is S.P. Stanley and all ID and credit cards will be in the Range Rover.

Before Sam left for his trip to Nebraska, he received confirmation that Susan and Andrew would love to join him on his trip to Europe.

The summer term ended and all the teacher's said there farewells, Sam returned to the boat, packed and was on his way to the airport in LA.

He arrived at the airport parked the car in long term and checked himself in on flight number DA 132 direct flight to Kansas City.

CHAPTER 46

Three hours later Sam landed in Kansas City, checked through Customs and collected his Land Rover and drove the three hour journey to the Motel in Lincoln Nebraska. The countryside was pure agriculture with cornfields stretching for miles. He stopped in the middle of nowhere to inspect the contents in the boot and found all to be satisfactory. One Heckler and Koch PSG 1 Sniper rifle, together with 200 rounds of 7.62 x 51mm Nato cartridges. An M1/M3 Infrared night sighting device which was known as a Sniperscope. This scope would be perfect for working in a dence wooded area, using the infrared light force to illuminate targets. Having satisfied himself with the contents in the boot, he proceeded on towards Lincoln, Nebraska.

The girl was expecting him at the reception desk

'Welcome to Nebraska Mr. Stanley, are you going to take some pictures of our lovely State

'I sure hope so,' said Sam.

He showered, shaved and changed and went down to dinner, he noticed an attractive lady sitting at the bar and decided that it was Sally Powers.

Miss Powers had been briefed on the arrival of S.P. Stanley, she made her way towards Sam's table and dropped a note down on the table top. She had confirmed that the "Nigger Hunt" would take place on Wednesday next, starting out at Lincoln forest east, and that the black youth had been informed of this. So Sam had three days to organise a shooting area. He studied the map of the Lincoln F marked the set off point on the map and decided the location where he would make his stand.

The timing for the Wednesday had to be perfect, so Sam laid it out, 0800 hours the youth would set out on his five mile trek through the forest, 0815 hours the hunting party would set off in pursuit of the black youth, Sam would be in position one mile into the forest dead centre. Sally Powers would complete the last harvest and make her way to Kansas City and the debriefing location. 0900 hours the FBI would move in and take control of the set off area and the actual farm.

By 0700 hours on the Wednesday Sam was in his central position approximately a mile in from the northern end of the forest. At 0800 the black lad was let loose amid cheers from the hunters, and after a lapse of 5 minutes the hunters started off after there prey. An hour later the black youth was picked up by Sam, moving swiftly through the undergrowth, this kid was a true athlete thought Sam. Sam picked up the leading pursuers and lined them up on the cross hairs. Two shots in 6 seconds saw one of the hunter's yell in agony as a hole as big as a fist appeared at the rear of his shoulder, his partner in crime collapsed after a round hit him in the thigh. Sam scanned the area to the right of the two fallen hunter's and two bright yellow images came up, slowly making there way towards the black youth. Sam put a round into one of the guys thigh and severed the left ear of his hunting partner. Two of the hunter's had heard the cries of there brother's and called out that they had had enough and were returning to the set off area. Before taking care of the final two Nazi hunter's Sam got on he radio to inform the bureau lads that two of the hunter's had given up and were returning to the set off area. The final two hunter's were not going to give up and were closing in fast on the mark, Sam spotted the two of them working in tandem 300 yards away in a heavily wooded area. He squeezed off two rounds one hitting the shoulder of the lead hunter and the second a split second later a bullet crashing into the second guys groin area. Sam got on the radio informing the FBI lads that the raiding hunter's had been nulified and that he was withdrawing to collect the black youth.

Sam reached the northern end rendesvue point at more or less the same time as the young black youth, took him on board and left him with the main group of bureau personnel at the setting off area. After a final check and all the Nazi hunter's safely either in custody or hospital bound, Sam left for the de-brief in Kansas City. Sam checked in the Holiday Inn in the south of the city and joined Sally to complete the de-brief for the FBI. Sam phoned the General at the Pentagon confirmed a successful mission and made his way to the airport to return to his home in Santa Barbara.

CHAPTER 47

Sam had put the following arrangements in place prior to leaving for the Greyhound Bus Terminal to meet up with Susan and Andrew. He had reserved two rooms in Miami, one double for Susan and Andy and a single for himself, he also confirmed the sleeping arrangements with Lance at the Manor. The Greyhound powered its way to Los Angeles Airport where the three of them checked in for the flight to Miami. After an uneventful flight they set down in Miami and took a courtesy bus to the nearby Holiday Inn. The following morning they boarded the British Airways flight direct to London, Heathrow. The cabin crew were excellent and spoiled them all the way across the Atlantic, even managing to let Andy have a brief visit to the cockpit of the aircraft and a chat with the pilot. Sam woke both Susan and Andy as the undercarriage dropped on the huge plane, informing them that they had arrived in the UK.

They all cleared Customs and Immigration and were just leaving the arrivals area when Sam spotted Lance standing with jhis two daughters holding up a sign reading Lassiter. Introductions were made all round and they all climbed aboard Lance's giant Bentley. Just over an hour later Lance pulled into the drive of Sunningdale Estate.

'Welcome to my home Susan and Andy,' said Lance.

Simpson and two other man servants helped with the baggage as the three of them were ushered to there rooms in the west wing of the Manor.

Lance, his wife and two daughters, Susan and Andy, and Sam sat in the beautiful dining room and ate a wonderful meal. Topped off of course with Lance's favourite tipple, an ice cold chablis.

The holiday was going really well with Sam busy grass cutting and showing Andy all the goings on at the Sunningdale Estate, and Susan forming a friendship with Lance's wife Yvonne. They both went on a shopping spree to London and took in the sights of the famous city. Sam suggested to Lance that the two girls should go to Paris, he new that it was a dream for Susan.

'Good idea Sam,' said Lance, who proceeded to book the girls on a flight to Paris.

While Susan was away in Paris, Sam took Andy to the Planetarium in London, this was the highlight of Andy's visit to Europe, and on his return to the Manor asked if he could re-visit.

'Give it a couple of days Andy and we will take your Mum as well'.

It was the final week of the grass harvest and just one more week of the Summer entertainment at the Manor, a time for maintenance and a general clear up of the place. The end of summer dance open to all employees on the estate was on Saturday, Katherine and her new beau would be there, but Trisha couldn't make it. Sam took the Allard with Andy and drove to Camberley to meet Trisha and for Andy to meet his pen pal Thomas. It was lovely to see Trisha again and also witness a true friendship developing between Andy and Thomas.

'I've met a nice fella Sam, he's a Captain in the REME based here in Camberley, he is a very quiet man and a true gentleman, I think we can make it together,'

'I am so pleased for you Trish, if anybody deserves a happy ending you do', said Sam.

After tea and sandwiches Sam and Andy said there goodby's and left for Sunningdale and to meet up with Susan and Yvonne who had just returned from Paris.

It was the final evening meal at the Manor as Sam, Susan and Andy were leaving the next morning for there long journey back home to Southern California. Sam excused himself and at Andy's request carried him all the way to his bedroom on his shoulders. As soon as Andy's head hit the pillow he was out for the count, so after tucking him in Sam returned to the dining room for a nice brandy nightcap. After a general good night everybody left the dining room, Lance and family directly to bed, which left Sam alone with Susan.

'Do you fancy a walk in the gardens Sam,'

'Yeh lets do it,'

It was a typical English late summer balmy evening as they both wandered through the lovely gardens of Sunningdale Manor.

'It's not working for me Sam, I have tried so hard to make it work but I still have problems with your extra curicular activities, I can't come to terms with the killing and violence even though you have told me that these people are vermin. I really have tried so hard with this but I can't accept it, so when we get back home I think we should call it a day on any possible romance,'

'It's not a problem Susan, ok it's going to hurt like hell for a while, but I had an idea two weeks ago that this was going to happen so I telephoned your child carer and told her to collect all your belongings from the boat and take them to your apartment,'

'I would still very much like you to be my friend and of course if you agree still go to see Andy every Sunday afternoon.'

'I wouldn't have it any other way,' said Susan.

Lance's driver took Sam's party to the airport and they checked in for the the flight to Los Angeles, via Chicago.

The trip home must have been the longest and most boring Sam had ever had, no conversation with Susan and limited words with Andy. Sam wondered if he had guessed that something was amiss between him and his Mother.

At last they landed in LA, took the Greyhound to Santa Barbara said there goodbies and took separate taxi's to there homes.

CHAPTER 48

The term up to Christmas was running smoothly and Sam was enjoying the challenge, anytime in his life when things were not going to well Sam threw all his energy into his work and studies. . . He thought his delivery was improving and was contributing more at evening and day release classes at teacher's college. He changed his seating position at the college well away from Susan in an effort not to put her or himself under unessessary pressure.

His 38th birthday came and went, he did bring a few cakes to the staff room to keep up the tradition. The evening he spent on board the "Jon Jo" with a good book.

Goleta under 14 soccer side was playing some good stuff, showing quality in every department, defence, midfield and with classy strikers up front. They had progressed to the finals of the under 15 California Cup which was a fantastic achievement considering that all player's were 14 and under.

Two hundred fans turned up to watch the boys at the semi-final stage on the Saturday, the match was against the favourites for the cup Saint Augustus High. They looked twice the size of Sam's team as they made there way on to the field as they did there warm up.

Sam called his team together for a team talk.

'They are big but they are slow, expect long balls probably through the middle, so we will go with a sweeper, any balls over the top will be taken care of by Alonso. I want you to play two touch fast football and pass them off the park,'

It was well into the second half when a large youth from Augustus charged through two Goleta defenders fouled the goalkeeper and smashed the ball into the goal. Sam couldn't believe that the goal stood as it was a blatant foul on the Goleta keeper. The referee was booed and looked extremely embarrassed. Five minutes before the end of the second half Arturo scored a wonder goal and the whole of the Goleta followers roared with delight. An extra three minutes was being played when Arturo again burst through two tackles and sent the ball towards the goal, where one of the defenders stopped the ball with his hand. A clear cut penalty which Henry Ackerman our biggest and strongest player moved forward and placed the ball on the penalty spot. The whistle went and Henry moved forward and smashed the ball into the roof of the net. As the final whistle went all the Goleta kids sunk to there knees exhausted.

Sam collected the team around him and said.

'That was the most professional performance I have every witnessed, well done, see you all tomorrow, get some good sleep in,' said Sam.

The final on the following day was a bit of a miss match as Sam's Goleta side swarmed all over the Corinthians middle school and were three goals up at half time. Sam's half time talk was keep it as it is, two touch and don't let them have any posession. Goleta ran out the winners's by 7-0 and collected the cup. Sam congratulated the team and then shook hands with the coach of the young Corinthian side.

'Ok get showered and then on the bus, we are off to Goleta high for a celebration party,' said Sam.

Sam navigated his way through all the parents of the players and thanked them for there support over the whole season.

After the euphoria of the cup win things settled down nicely as Sam sat in his desk as 2a filtered into the classroom. He noticed that Timothy Foster was moving slowly head bowed and limping.

'Are you ok Tim,' said Sam

'I'm ok sir, I fell down the stairs at home, just a few bruises,'

'Let me have a look Tim,'

Sam realised that Tim was hiding something and suggested he go to see Nurse Carroll in First Aid, Sam would talk to the nurse later as he was not convinced that young Tim was telling the truth, or to frightened to.

When the lesson finished Sam went along to see Nurse Carroll.

'He didn't fall down the stairs Sam, these bruises were inflicted by a third person,'

'Leave it to me Nurse, I'll have a word with Mrs. Foster after school,' said Sam.

4pm came and Sam stood in the student collecting area watching the parents collect there children, he spotted Mrs. Foster hurrying young Tim to her vehicle.

'Excuse me Mrs. Foster I'm not satisfied with Tim's explanation that all the bruising he has was due to him falling down the stairs, they look like a third party has caused the injuries, I am considering reporting the excess bruising to the Principal who will take it further to the relevant authorities.

'Please Mr. Lassiter, my husband is getting treatment for his problem and is showing signs of getting to grips with it,'

'I'll be monitoring the situation very closely and if I ever see any further bruising from an attack by your waste of space husband, I'll come a calling and it won't be pleasant,' said Sam.

Tim didn't appear at school for a week, and Sam was getting worried so he approach Principal Clark and put her in the picture.

'That's a serious assumption Sam, if I report this we must be full proof,'

'I understand that, if this guy is still hurting young Tim I think maybe a little payback is due,' said Sam.

Tim returned to school eight days later and Sam could see the remains of bruises on his arms and legs, he would meet Mrs. Foster after school.

He SUV pulled into the pick-up area and she collected Tim, Sam saw that a man was sitting in the passenger side of the vehicle.

'That man of yours has been at it again hasn't he?' said Sam

'He is trying so hard Mr. Lassiter, but it's not working,'

Sam strode over to the SUV very angry, opened the door and yanked out Mr. Foster by the scruff of his neck, he delivered a hard punch to the solar plexis and a second blow to the jaw, Foster went down like a sack of coke half in and half out of the SUV.

Sam looked towards Mrs. Foster and said,

'Get this heap of crap out of here and when he comes around tell him that he will be going to court,'

Sam was watched by many of the parents who were picking up there childen as he retired to the staff room to cool down, he was very angry. The teachers said well done to Sam, but Sam had reservations that he may have gone to far and ruined his chances of becoming a full time qualified teacher.

CHAPTER 49

A week after the incident in the student pick-up area Sam received a court summons to appear at 10am on 27th September, 1960 charged with common assault. He had a conversation with Principal Clark who granted him time off to prepare for the court case.

'Not required Ma'am, just take care of my lessons please on that Thursday,' said Sam.

One thing in Sam's favour was that Foster had been found guilty of child abuse the day before Sam's case, and received a six months sentence and ordered to continue his Anger Management classes.

The courtroom was full to capacity when Judge Ruth Steinman entered the court.

'All rise,' came the call from the court clerk.

'Where is you legal council Mr. Lassiter,' said the judge,

'I'll conduct my own defence such as it is your honour.'

'Ok Mr. Prosecutor what have you got, lets proceed,' said the judge.

'At approximately 4pm on the 7th September Mr. Lassiter dragged my client out of his car and hit him many times until he was unconsious, he then left the scene and left it to two school janitors to help

Mr. Foster. Mr. Foster refused any help from the ambulance service, struggled into Mrs. Fosters SUV and left the area, He did go to the hospital that same evening to have his fractured nose straightend.

Sam got to his feet.

'Your Honour, you asked why I did not have legal council, well it's because I have no defence, it is what you American's call a "Slam Dunk" I did hit him three times, with what are called pulled punches,'

'What are pulled punches Mr.Lassiter?' said the judge.

'It's when a blow is delivered at less power, the punch is pulled to lessen the impact, your honour,'

Before I sit down your honour can I stress that my actions were purely personal and had nothing to do with the high principle's of Goleta Junior High,'

'Duly noted,' said the judge.

'Any further comments from the prosecution,' said the judge.

'Why this attack from Mr. Lassiter was so violent can be put down to three major things, one he has a black belt in karate, two a black belt in Judo and is well versed in unarmed combat.'

'Is that true Mr. Lassiter,' said judge Steinman,

'Yes Ma'am a two Dan in both karate and judo, and well up in unarmed combat due to my time in WW2 in the Royal Marines.'

'I'm not to sure of the law in the USA, but in the UK my hands would be regarded as lethal weapons, so perhaps you can understand the reason for me pulling punches, your honour,'

'Ok I've heard enough Mr. Lassiter you have got to stop hitting people, this court finds you guilty. You will serve 100 hours of Community Service at the Youth Criminal Establishment here in Santa Barbara, case closed.'

Sam lingered behind sorting out his hours of community service work with the court clerk, while Foster resplendent in his orange overalls was escorted out of the court room and back to prison.

CHAPTER 50

Sam was pleased that he was not romantically involved at the moment because with his present workload there is no way he good give any lady due care and attention. A full days teaching at Goleta High Monday through Thursday, college Monday and Wednesday evenings, and a day release at college on a Friday. His community service hours were 6 on Tuesday, Thursday and Saturday and 6 hours on Sundays after his visits to Andy.

On the Friday at college he was asked what it was like at the Juvenile Detention Centre by one of the teaching instructors.

'In a word heart breaking, some of these kids will never be released to the outside world, the lads that have commited murder will graduate to an adult prison be moved on to death row and await the call to the Chair or Lethal Injection. I would never wish any child to be in a place like a juvenile Detention establishment.

'It's very sad,' said Sam sitting down and bowing his head. An uneasy quiet decended on the whole staffroom.

During the last week of Sam's time at the Centre he was on mobile watch with his mentor when he noticed a young lad with his head buried into a book.

'Good to see,' said Sam,

'Not really the kid is posing he can't read at all,'

Sam walked over to the youth, eyed his name tag and said,

'How would you like to learn to read young man?'

'Can you teach me?' said Damon.

'I can try, move over,' said Sam.

Sam started the long process of getting the right sound of the various letters, running through the alphabet from A to Z.

As Sam and Damon progressed a few of the passing inmates were showing interest.

'Don't be shy gentlemen come and sit down and listen,'

After an hour of constant reference to the alphabet and the sound of the letters, Sam decided enough was enough for a first session.

'Sunday morning we continue, that's if you are up for it,' said Sam.

It was Saturday morning when Sam landed at the bookshop in the Santa Barbara Mall, he bought 20 books entitled "Learn to read made easy".

When he arrived at the detention centre on the Sunday morning he was greeted with 16 inmates all ready to attend his teach in. He distributed the books and motioned to Damon to stand up and give it a go. He stumbled through the first text 'The cat sat on the mat, he liked this as it was warm and comfy,'

'I think applause is called for gentlemen,' said Sam

The other lads clapped there hands vigourously.

The remainder of the lesson went well with so many questions for Sam to answer.

'Ok that's it for today guys, on Tuesday next I'll be expecting big things from you, so work hard,'

It was halfway through the afternoon session on the Friday a week later, when the Principal entered Sam's classroom and had a quiet word in the Instructor's ear.

He stood in the centre of the stage and said,

'Ladies and Gentlemen I'm sure you are aware of Mr.Lassiter's court case and the subsequent course of action. I have received today a letter from the Governor of the Santa Barbara Juvenile Correction Centre, it reads,

Since Mr Lassiter has been with us, thats approximately 3 weeks, he has instigated a "Teach yourself to read programme, this programme has proved to be very successful, starting with 3 inmates it now has 26 all keen to learn to read. Since it's inseption the trouble and violence at the centre has subsided. All the teaching staff at your college should be proud of there achievements in producing teacher's of such high quality as Mr. Lassiter. Regards Alexander Sterling, Governor,'

Amid thunderous clapping the Principal shouted 'Well done Sam,'

'Time for a mid lesson coffee, I think,' said the Instructor.

The whole of the class adjourned to the cafeteria, with everybody wanting to congratulate Sam.

The Michaelmas term at Goleta was meandering along which was great for Sam and his huge workload, Four full days at the chalkface at Goleta High, two evenings a week night school, one day a week day release for teacher training college and ten hours a week "Teach yourself to read" classes at the Correction Centre. It's was a relief that Sam was not romantically involved at this time, because it would never work as Sam was perpetually tired.

It was Thursday late afternoon as Sam was making his way along the central corridor towards his final class of the day with 2a, when he heard two gun shots coming from the direction of the staff room, there were kids running everywhere.

'What's happening' Sam asked a fleeing student,

'Roberto Valasques old man going crazy with a gun sir,'

'Where' said Sam

'Teacher's staff room,' said another fleeing student,,

Sam now sprinting crashed through the staff room door, and saw a hispanic pointing a gun at Principal Clark, he got within two yards of the man and launched himself into a rugby type diving tackle, as he cannoned into the hispanic guy the gun sounded and Sam felt searing pain in his left shoulder. Sam hit the guy so hard in the solar plexis that he went backwards and his head struck the corner of a desk and ne was out cold, the gun skidding across the floor and coming to rest at the feet of a shaking Principal Clark.

Sam stood up over the slumped body of Mr. Valasques blood running from his shoulder leaking onto his left hand and forming a dark red puddle on the floor.

The Principal then took command calling for the Police and an ambulance, she then called the school nurse to attend to Sam.

Within ten minutes the perpetrator was cuffed and on his way to the cells and Sam was on his way to Santa Barbara General Hospital.

A few stitches and a dressing and Sam was sitting up in bed reviewing next weeks teaching programme.

His first visitor was Sharon Clark, she sat down in a chair by Sam's bed.

'How are you feeling Sam,'

'A bit sore but I've had worse,' he said,

'Thank you for saving my life Sam,'

'It's not a problem Ma'am, who would keep me in order if you were not around,'

The Head Nurse poked he head around the door of Sam's room and said.

'I've got twenty kids in the waiting area wanting to see Mr. Lassiter,'

Sam put on a dressing gown and walked to the waiting room and met with the entire class of 2c.

'Ok guys I'm alright I'll see you next Monday.' Happy that there favourite teacher was ok they drifted out of the emergengy waiting room and made there way home.

Sam signed himself out the following morning took a cab to the boat, washed and shaved and climbed into his car and set off for day release at the college.

He sat down more or less in the front left hand corner of the lecture room amid calls of are you ok from the majority of the class.

'I'm fine thanks,' said Sam.

Halfway through the lecture Professor Clayton the top man interupted the lecture.

'Can I have your attention please ladies and gentlemen,'

'Yesterday was one of the blackest moments in the history of Santa Barbara, alongside Mr. Lassiter's brush with death at Goleta High, we had an even worse situation at Columbia college, a man burst into a class room and shot dead a teacher and four pupils. If any of you potential teacher's heve any doubts about being a member of this proffesion now is the time to air your thoughts,'

Most of the ladies present said although they were not completely at ease with the situation decided to return to college next term to complete the degree course and receive there diploma's. Sam was slightly takeb aback with Susan's reply when she said that no drugged up mainiac was going to stop her obtaining was going to stop her obtaining something she has always wanted, a teaching degree.

'Ok lets here from Sam as he experianced the incident at Goleta,'

Sam stood and was beckened over to the what looked like a preachers podium.

'Twenty years ago I was fighting the Japanese in Burma with the British Royal Marines so I know what violence is, after five years of jungle warfare I left the Marines and travelled to the USA and was recruited by the Pentagon as a trouble shooter, so more violence. I changed my name and became a natralised American and therefore responsible to American law,'

'Two amendments to the Constitution I didn't understand, firstly the 5th Amendment, what a load of rubbish, if it were a European court that answer "I plead the fifth" would be taken as guilty.'

'The sccond amendment, the right to bear arms also needs a good look at by congress, over 90 million hand guns are out there in the USA, most of them in the hands of people of below average intellegance. And the powers that be wonder why the murder rates are up in most cities. America has got to work towards ensuring only the Forces and crime prevention personnel are the only people aloud to posess fire arms. This of course will never happen, One day in the not to distant future a guy is going to walk into a crowded school, college or university and massacre many people with a machine pistol, and still the Congress won't move on tighter legislation.

Sam returned to his seat nodding to the class who were applauding and quietly whispering "here here".

'So there you have it, my office door is always open for you, if you want to come along for a talk please do so, no appointment necessary.' said Professor Clayton.

At the end of the day Sam slipped into the gents toilet and took a pain killer, to relieve the dull ache in his shoulder. He walked to the car park to find Susan standing next to his Dino .

'Hi are you ok,' said Sam

'Not really Sam, I really have been a stupid woman in leaving you twice, I've been thinking a lot about it and would like very much to be part of your life again,'

'You dumped me twice Susan, the last time left me in bits and I can't take a chance on you doing it again, that would really screw me up big time. So the answer is no, you will always be a beautiful lady and I hope you can be a good friend, it won't take long for you to find a good man, a quiet man, a man not linked with violence. I will still visit Andy if that is fine with you, but there will never be any romance for us.'

'Good by, beautiful lady,' said Sam sliding into his Ferrari and heading off in the direction of the marina.

CHAPTER 51

The following Saturday it was the end of term night out for all the would be teacher's at Santa Barbara Teaching College, a few of the girls arranged an evening at a Spanish Bar in the city, husbands, wives, girlfriends and boyfriends were welcome.

Sam called Monique who said she would love to come along to the party. As he would be taking out one of the most glamorous ladies in southern california, Sam put in an effort to look as good as possible. A charcoal grey Georgio Armani suit, a tailor made silk dark grey shirt and Italian shoes. He called on Monique who glided towards the Ferrari like she was walking a cat walk, she looked stunning wearing the same Dior dress that she wore to the film premier months before. A white low cut, off one shoulder number with a split from the floor to her waist revealing a long slendour sunburned leg.

'That dress doesn't leave much to the imagination "Spud", I hope you have got some knickers on,' said Sam

'Yes knickers on but very tiny, but no bra,' said Monique laughing.

It was a 100% turn out for the end of term party at the Spanish Bar, the hosts Professor Clayton and his lovely wife Jill did the meeting and greeting.

Monique wandered around the bar and as usual a camera dangling from around her neck, introducing herself and taking a lot of photographs. This kid wasn't shy he told himself as he sat down at a vacant table after collecting a variety of tapas from the bar.

'You have an admirer young man,' said a voice that Sam didn't recognise,

'Ah Mrs. Clayton I didn't realise it was you,' said Sam

'That pretty girl sitting over there can't keep her eyes off of you,' said Jill Clayton,

'We had a thing going for a while, it seemed to be just fine until I was a bit tardy with my housework, I left a crunched up letter from the Pentagon in my waste basket congratulating me on a successful mission in Memphis. She of course read it, tracked it back a the local library noting the carnage that had occurred, she put two and two together and arrived at four, she confronted me head on and said that she had a problem handling my extra curricular activities and thought it would be a good idea not to see each other,' said Sam

'I think she will have you back again now Sam,' said Mrs. Clayton

'I was in bits the last time she told me to go, it's not going to happen again Ma'am.

'My name is Jill, by the way, let's dance Sam.

Half way through a slow foxtrot Sam got a tap on the shoulder,

'Can we do a trade Mr. Lassiter', said the Professor offering Monique before taking his wife in his arms to complete the dance.

The dance concluded and the band announced that they would be taking a 10 minute break.

Sam sat down at a table with Monique, she seemed to be very happy talking to anybody who would listen and taking hundreds of photographs.

'I'll have to take you out more often "Spud" I haven't seen you so happy for a long time,' said Sam

'I've loved every minute of being out with you Sam,' she said with what looked like a bit of a blush.

Monique and Sam found an empty table and sat down nursing a couple of sahara dry martini's, they were joined at the table by Professor Clayton and his wife Jill.

'Sam when you get your teaching degree in three months time I want you to join the teaching staff here at Santa Barbara College, what do you say,' said the Professor.

'Reluctantly I say no sir, I owe the Principal at Goleta High for giving me the opportunity to teach and I have loved every minute of it, I progressed from soccer coach to a temporary history and geography teacher prior to attending your wonderful college I prefer to teach the kids who have learning difficulties, when they finally understand what I'm talking about it's like a breath of fresh air to me,' said Sam.

'Will you still be carrying on with your "Learning to Read" programme at the young offenders detention centre Sam,' said Jill Clayton.

'Very much so, we are recruiting new reading teacher's as we speak here,' said Sam.

'Finally Sam, I won't give up in enticing you away from Goleta High, you should know that,' said the Professor with a smile,

'I'm flattered sir,' said Sam.

At 1am the party finished and people were standing in line to collect there coats, Susan came over to Sam and said,

'I have been looking at you all night trying to catch your attention, but you seem to be ignoring me,' said Susan,

'You really don't understand do you what you did to me when you told me that our romance was over, for Christs sake you crippled me, and I'll tell you something Susan it aint going to happen again. The only occasional contact we have in the future is when I visit Andy on a Sunday afternoon. We are not an item and we never will be,' said Sam.

Monique arrived then and they collected there coats and left the building.

'I hope my birth is clean and tidy Sam, I'm staying on board tonight,'

'Clean as a whistle, just don't snore to loud,' said Sam.

CHAPTER 52

They reached the "Jon Jo" separated and went to there cabins to change, Sam returned to the upper lounge and prepared two night caps. He was dressed as usual in his night gear of shorts and a T shirt.

'Where is that white towelling dressing gown colonel Sam,'

'Hanging on my door in my cabin,' replied Sam

Sam carried the two martini's to the low coffee table, sat on the sofa and waited for Monique to arrive. She entered the lounge completely naked and carrying the dressing gown, walked across to the sofa, sat down and pulled on the white robe.

'The last time I saw you naked you were twelve years old skinny dipping in Burma,' said Sam

'I've probably filled out a bit since then,' said Monique.

'You could say that and you've washed your face too,' said Sam.

Monique slid across close to Sam and placed her head on his lap and within minutes was fast asleep. Sam gently placed a cushion under her head, covered her with a duvet and went off to his cabin.

The following morning Sam went to the galley to make some coffee, slipped quietly into the lounge to wake up Monique. No need she had already left, folded the duvet neatly and left a note saying that she had lots to do and would be in contact.

CHAPTER 53

Sam set out his workload for the final three days of term and then set about the programme for the forthcoming Easter term. He had six "Great Lives" to prepare, so he sat down to select some famous great characters of history. He selected Napoleon, General McArthur, Anne Frank, Frank Mitchell, Shindler and the Dam Busters. He went ino the US Postal and copied portraits of the chosen late and greats. He returned to the boat and started writing there lfe stories.

The last three days of term ambled to a close, all the kids shouted there goodby's and wished him a happy Christmas.

Sam packed up all his stuff and was just leaving the classroom when he was stopped by Principal Clark,

'Can you give us a hand on Friday Sam to help decorate the assembly hall for the end of term Christmas Dance for all the staff at Goleta,'

'Of course Ma'am, what time,' said Sam.

'Four in the afternoon would be good,'

'I'll be there,'

Sam got back to the boat and gave Monique a call.

'End of term Christmas dance at Goleta High on Saturday are you up for that,' said Sam'

'You mean you are actually asking me out on a date,' said Monique,

'It's not a date more of a company thing,'

'I would love to come out with you not on a date Sam,'

'Ok, I'll call 7.30 pm Saturday at your place, don't wear that white dress, some of the old boys could have a heart attack.

'Don't worry I'll come in my Nun's outfit,' she said hanging up the phone.

Sam arrived at the school gym at 4pm and started moving the hired white tables into position around what was to become a dance floor, he placed white table cloths on all the tables and set a vase ready to except a posy of roses that were to be delivered the following day. More volunteers showed up and in no time the place was transformed. The final operation was to polish the floor in the dancing area which Sam did with the automatic polisher.

'Ok folks that's about it, see you all tomorrow dressed in your Saturday best.' said Principal Clark.

The vision of beauty that greeted Sam at the door of Studio Monique was stunning, she was wearing a very short black simple dress designed by Michael Kors, one strap over each shoulder, low cut top and a hem line a full 4 inches above the knee, emphasizing her long slendour shapely legs and of course the Leica 35mm camera dangling from around her neck.

Sam and Monique arrived at the school and settled in a seat away from the immediate action, Monique nursing an orange juice and Sam a bottle of local beer.

Principal Clark came over to Sam's table and sat down and was soon in deep conversation with Monique about fashion and photography in the world of show business.

'A far cry from my business Monique,'

'But not so awarding as your vocation Sharon,' said Monique.

'I shall be circulating the party and taking as many photo's as I can and I'll get them to you Sharon via Sam.

'Wonderful,' said Sharon Clark.

The evening was grand all the guests mixing nicely, proving to Sam that it was the right move to stay with the Goleta High school and not leave to pursue Teaching the Teacher's at Professor Clayton's college. Midnight came and many of the guests started to leave, Sam and Monique collected there coats and were just leaving when they met a worried looking Principal Clark.

'There is a huge problem up at the Juvenile Detention Centre, one of the lads a Joey Patterson is sitting with his legs dangling over the edge of the building four stories up and threatening to jump if he is not allowed to talk with Sam,'

'Tell the Police and the Centre I'm on my way, come on "Spud" lets move it,' said Sam.

They arrived at the Centre and Sam immediatley took the lift to the 6th floor, where he encountered two Detectives and four prison Wardens not knowing wether to stick or twist.

'Hi everybody my name is Sam Lassiter I work here and Joey is one of my better students, so could you please all vacate this area and let me see what I can do,'

Sam moved on to the roof of the building and stopped 10 yards away from Joey Patterson.

'Hi Joe, silly question. How are you doing,'

'Not to good Sam, you shouldn't have taught me to read,'

'Yeh, and why is that,' said Sam

'You know next year I graduate for want of a better word to a adult male prison, well, I've just finished reading the biography of convicted murderer Wayne Givens who was recently released after 30 years in the slammer, he was consistantly male raped and made to do things he had only seen in homosexual porn movies. He made it through all that but is a very changed and bitter old man. I won't be able to cope with that Sam, so it's best if I end it all,'

He eased forward a little so that only the tip of his rear end was on the roof surrounding wall.

Sam noticed that the Police had set up the inflatable landing bubble more or less beneath where Joey was perched on the end of the building.

'Can I come over closer to you Joey I don't like shouting and I don't want the police to know our business, and if I do promise me you won't take me over with you, I've still got a lot of living to do and so do you,'

Sam was now sitting on the little wall right alongside Joey and continued his dialogue.

'i've been talking to a Lawyer friend of mine a guy called Gerry Anderson, he is quite a famous character, he takes on cases pro-bono that he thinks the verdict stinks and a miscarriage of justice was made, he reviewed your case and he wants to take it on. This guy is a winner Joey, give him a chance buddy,'

'Why are you doing all this for me Sam, you hardly know me,'

'Because I probably would have done the same thing as you did when you killed that bastard for hurting your Mum and sister.'

They both stepped back over the wall on to the roof, Joey held out his arms and Sam moved in with a bear hug and they both made there way to the safety of the elevator and took it to the bottom floor. Joey wouldn't let go of Sam as they passed by the Police, Wardens and TV camera's and led him into an Ambulance for a check up.

Sam sought out the Governor of the Centre and suggested 24/7 surveillance on Joey and that he would be requesting some private time with Joey Patterson and the Lawyer Gerry Anderson in the near future.

'You've got it Sam and well done, nice job,' said the Governor of the Centre.

Sam brushed the waiting media aside and made his way to Monique who was waiting anciously by the Ferarri.

'What are you some kind of madman, going up and sitting next to a kid who is about to jump to his death and take you with him, don't you think people will miss you too, people like me,'

'Relax and get in the car, I need a drink, a strong one,' said Sam.

Not a word was spoken on the journey back to the boat, Sam could see that Monique was angry as she got out of the car and went straight to her jeep and drove off into the night.

CHAPTER 54

Monique had calmed down a little when she phoned the next day inviting Sam to Christmas lunch at Doctor Jon's house, it will be just you and me plus Manuel's family as my brother is in Tokyo with his wife mixing a bit of a holiday in between business.

It was Christmas Eve when Sam pulled into the car park at Doctor Kramer's Clinic, 9pm and it was lights out for all the patients. He signed in and made his way to the conservatory where Andy had set up the damaged telescope and locked on to the "Milky Way", Sam stripped all the damaged parts off the scope and replaced them with the new parts that he had purchased as a Christmas present for Andy. It took him two hours to complete the repairs and to re-set the tracking of the camera. After he had signed himself out he made his way to the main exit and bumped into Susan and her new man who was carrying many gift wrapped presents.

'Merry Christmas to both of you,' said Sam as he left for his car.

The Christmas meal was beautifly prepared by Manuel, after which presents were given out and everybody relaxed in the upper lounge. Manuel and his family departed for there own quarters and left Monique and Sam alone. Monique stretched her long slim frame out laying down on the giant sofa and resting her head in Sam's lap. It wasn't long before she was fast asleep and away with the fairies. Sam let her sleep for a half an hour then gently eased her off his lap, put a cushion under her head and quietly left the Li home.

The next few days were spent in preparation for next term, history and geography, soccer schedules, great lives presentations and his learning to read programme for the lads at "Juve".

Three weeks into the new term Sam was sitting in the top lounge of the boat marking some paper's when he noticed his lawyer friend Gerry Anderson on the TV, he increased the volume to hear Gerry say that justice has been done and that lifer Joey Patterson's life sentence had been reduced to 5 to 15 years. This means he continued that Joey would be sent to an open prison when he reached adulthood and would be up for parroll in two years.

Sam immediately called Gerry and thanked him for a wonderful job.

The first few weeks of the 1961 Easter Term was passing nicely with no majoe incidences, everything in the garden was roses.

He was sitting at a spare desk in the staff room marking some late papers from 2a, when he glanced up at the TV which was flashing in and out of signal, he picked up on a conversation with an old lady who was complaining that there was a shortage of skilled labour in the Santa Barbara area, especially carpenter's and plumbers. She said she had to search far and wide to get some jobs done in her condo.

This sparked an idea into Sam's mind, what if we at the "Juve" engaged a couple of skilled men and taught the lads the fundementals in carpentry and plumbing.

He immediately phoned the Governor at the Detention Centre and pitched his idea.

'I like it Sam, but things are tight at the moment with regard to funding, I can maybe come up with $50000,'

'Leave the pennies to me sir, I'll get back to you, just a thought the old restaurant building at the rear of the exercise yard, with a few adjustments would make a fine workshop,' said Sam,

'Excellent keep me in the loop Sam,'

Sam composed a letter to Jerry Brown the Governor of California outlining the proposed extention to the already very successful "Learn to Read" programme, by introducing basic skill training in specifically carpentry and plumbing. On completing there sentences the young men would heve some basic skill level. If the State of California could donate some kind of grant to this end it would be wonderful. Sam signed and posted the letter.

A week later much to Sam's surprise an official looking letter arrived in the post from the State of California. It read:

Dear Sam, Your letter got my interest, ever since your trial for giving that lout a belt around the ear I personally and my wife have kept an eye on you. I have had reports that you and the rest of the wardens at the Correction Centre are doing a fantastic job, especially with the introduction and success of the Learning to Read programme. I think the additioal learning of a practical skill is a good one and one that I could support, so I'll tell you what I'm prepared to do. Any dollars you can collect via Fund Raisers or the like, the

State of California will donate and match that amount, how does that sound Sam. Keep up the good work.

Regards

Jerry Brown

Governor of California.

Sam went straight to the phone and called Monique,

'I need your expertise "Spud" when can you come over,'

'Tonight 7.30 ish, is that ok?'

'Perfect,' said Sam replacing the phone in i'ts holder.

When Monique arrived Sam went through the whole thing, she loved the idea.

'So where do I come in,' she said

'I need 100 big hitters to attend a fund raiser, if we sell seats at $200 a pop, we are well on the way to our target. And don't forget Jerry said he would match me dollar for dollar,; said Sam.

'I can do that, but it will cost you dinner at Filippo's right now,'

'Deal,' said Sam.

Sam was very fortunate to have a special friend like Monique who was well acquainted with the majority of the heavy hitters in Film and fashion in Hollywood and within 3 hours she had 200 bums on seats at $200 a throw. The fundraiser would be held at the Holiday Inn in Santa Barbara the last Saturday in January,1961. The donated dollars would be for the conversion of the old disused restaurant in the Juvenile Correction Campus into a learning workshop, teaching the inmates the skills of using machines like lathes. Milling machines, grinders, along with woodworking skills. Trained machinists and woodworkers were hard to come by in

Southern California and it would be benificial to the lads on leaving the centre, trying to get a foot into life on the outside again.

The evening was a great success with all the big money people attending, it was nice to see Principal Clark and her husband there along with the Kramers. After a few drinks and light refreshments the Young Offenders Governor stood and delivered a little speech thanking everybody for coming and announcing that the total money received for the evening was $210000, a wonderful acheivement. He sat down to a round of polite applause.

After the cheering and clapping subsided the Toast Master introduced a surprise speaker that had only just arrived.

'Ladies and Gentlemen may I introduce you to Mrs. Jenny Brown the lovely wife of Governor Jerry Brown.' Everybody stood up and gave Jenny a resounding welcome as she stood alongside the microphone.

'Thank you so much, good evening, it's lovely to be here, my husband has been called to Washington DC for some conference or other and it's left to me to do the honours,'

'After Jerry had swapped correspondence with a young man called Sam Lassiter, they agreed to meet and immediately struck up a friendship, in so much as my man agreed that the State of California would match to match the take here dollar for dollar. So here is a cheque for $210000 as promised.' as she sat down to a thunderous round of applause she looked at Sam 'A few words Sam,'

'i'll adopt my usual after dinner speech procedure, stand up, speak up and shut up,' said Sam.

'just to say that you Americans are the most gener-
ous people in the world. By donating this money you'll
be giving some of these kids a chance in life to make
something of themselves, thank you all so much for
coming along and contributing so generously,' Again
loud noisy applause as Sam sat down.

For the rest of the evening Sam did his circulating
thing, danced with as many old ladies as he could
manage and pressed the flesh with nearly all the big
money men in the room. The final waltz started and
Sam looked around for Monique, he found her.

'You dancin,'

'You askin,'

'I'm askin,'

'I'm dansin.' she said.

'Thank you so much "Spud" you did it again for me,
you are a star,'

'Shut up and dance.'

CHAPTER 55

Work commenced really quick on the re-development of the old restaurant and within days the place was transformed. Nothing untoward was happening at Goleta High, or teacher's college except that Susan didn't show up for evening classes or day session on the Friday. Sam gave her a call, no reply, now he was a little worried he phoned Doctor Kramer to see if he new what was going on.

'Sam I was just going to call you, it's not good news about Susan, she has had x-rays and tests which indicate that she has contacted cancer, it is eating away at her kidneys and it is very severe, the specialists give her at best three months to live. She is not worried about herself she is aware that it is the end for her, but she is worried sick about what is going to happen to Andrew, her Mom and Dad are far to old to take this on, which means foster parents will have to be considered'

'Your very quiet Sam,'

'Devastated,' said Sam.

'You remember how beautiful she was, well she doesn't think she is any more, she is very thin she has lost a lot of weight he hair is falling out after kimo theraphy and she doesn't want to see anybody, especially you,' said the Doctor.'

'I don't give a shit whether she wants to see me or not, we must talk together about Andrew,' said Sam.

Sam drove straight to the hospital and made his way to the private ward where Susan was laying down and resting.

She woke as Sam sat down at her bedside and tried to cover up her thin tiny arms and ruffle up the bed clothes to give the impression that her legs were still the normal size and not skelital.

'I don't want you to see me like this Sam,'

'Don't be daft you will always be beautiful,'

'You are so kind but a dreadful liar Sam,'

'I am so worried about Andrew, I am not going to live very much longer the cancer is spreading like wild-fire, I can't bare the thought of him being transferred from foster parents to foster parents, he'll never make it, he will go back into fully fledged autism, the whole works,' said Susan through a downpour of tears.

'Mom and Dad are to old to take care of him fulltime and his Father has disowned him as you know, and I haven't enough money to pay for a full time nurse. I don't know what to do Sam.

'I do,' said Sam

'What?'

'Marry me, just because you kicked me out didn't stop me loving you Susan,'

'You are a wonderful man but I couldn't ask you to do that,' said Susan,

'It makes so much sense my love, you will be able to put your mind at rest knowing that I will give him the love and affection that you have given him for the last 12 years. I will be his official legal guardian, what do you say?'

'I say yes, yes, yes,'

'You rest now I'll be back later with a plan,' said Sam.

Sam made his way to Reception and asked an assistant to call a Priest from the Chapel and ask him to come along and see him. The priest agreed that he would carry out an emergency wedding at the bedside of Susan at 9pm that evening. Sam gave his thanks and made some phone calls to Susan's Mom and Dad, the Kramers and to Sharon Clark at Goleta High, he put them in the picture on what he intended to do and requested there company at Susan's bedside at 9pm that evening. The last contact was with the duty nurse assigned to Susan.

'Make her look like a million dollars nurse,' said Sam.

At 9pm all were assembled at Susan's bedside, Susan was sat up in bed and she looked thin but lovely, the nurse had done a fine job on her make up and what was left of her hair neatly woven into a little white hat.

The service was short and sweet and lovely, Sharon Clark broke down and was comforted by Doctor Kramer.

'I now pronounce yoy man and wife, you may kiss the bride,' said the Priest. Sam bent over and gently kissed Susan on the cheek.

'I love you,' he said

'I love you to you lovely man,' said Susan.

The witnesses signed the required papers, Sam thanked them and they left the two of them together.

'I'm so happy but very tired Sam,'

'Go to sleep and have a good rest, you did really well,' said Sam holding her hand very gently ensuring that none of her introvenous tubes were not damaged.

Sam drifted off to sleep after keeping his eyes on Susan for as long as he could and then about 3am he was wakened by a long continuous alarm from one of the many TV monitors, he stood up and cleared away from the bedside to allow the crash team free access to Susan, he left the area and sat in the waiting area, he could here orders being shouted between members of the crash team. Then silence, a silence he has witnessed many times during his service with the American Secret Service, the silence of death.

The Doctor appeared and was just about to part with the awful news, when Sam said 'Yes I know she's passed,'

'I'm so sorry Mr. Lassiter, we tried everything to save her,'

'I heard and saw you guys,you gave it better than your best shot.

The Kramer's, and all Susan's aquaintances were informed of her passing, it was left to Doctor Kramer to tell Andrew and let him know he had a new Guardian in Sam.

On the day of the funeral there was not one dry eye in the place, this lady was well loved. Sometimes Sam had to shake himself that there really is a god. Andrew didn't waver an inch away from Sam during the service and proved himself to be what Sam already new that the kid had courage.

Sam took over Susan's visiting slots as well as his own and Andrew was under the circumstances doing very well.

CHAPTER 56

The Easter term ended at Goleta and the final teacher's examination completed at college. Sam breezed through the exam, at last a fully fledged qualified teacher.

During one of Sam's Sunday visits to see Andrew, Doctor Kramer caught his eye.

'A word Sam,'

'Yes, hi Doc,' said Sam.

'I'm not sure you are aware of this Sam but every Tuesday visiting our Mr. Andrew has a very pretty lady visitor to see him, she has been coming along for the past month, they both seen engrossed in camera's,' said the Doctor.

'At this time with Susan no longer here she is doing a wonderful job with the lad, young lads need a Mum like figure and she is stepping up to the plate,'

'We are talking Monique here aren't we Doc?'

'Yes we are, I didn't believe anyone so busy with her photography and fashion business would have the time to spare ensuring that the kid was ok,'

'Monique Li, Doctor has a heart as big as a house,' said Sam.

One Sunday during Sam's visiting time with Andy, he said,

'I didn't know Monique was seeing you, how long has she been doing this,' said Sam,

'About 4 weeks, she just turned up sat down with me and started talking camera's, shutter speeds, lighting and general composition of photographs. She really knows what she is talking about.'

'Yes she does,' Sam agreed.'

'I think all the other boys look forward to her coming along as well as me, they tell me when she has left that she's a doll,' said Andy.

'You are definetly growing up to fast young man,' said Sam.

'Do you know what would be really cool Sam, that you, me and Monique could be a family, wouldn't that be fantastic,'

'Your halfway there already Andy. I'm your official guardian you know,'

'It was just a thought Sam,' said Andy.

'I'm a bit tired now I think I'll take my meds and have a little nap if thats ok with you,'

'Of course it is Andy, I'll see you soon,' said Sam.

As Sam was leaving he bumped into Doctor Kramer who said,

'Out of the mouth of every child sometimes comes a gem Sam, although it's none of my business the three of you would make a wonderful family,'

'I've not had much luck with family Doc, one died and one had a problem with my life outside teaching, so i'm not your ideal candidate.'

'You are so wrong with that statement young man, you are a great Dad to the lad already, Good night Sam, drive carefully in that bullet of a car and I'll see you soon,' said the Doctor.

CHAPTER 57

The next few months passed smoothly with Andrew responding well to his treatment and Sam spending the majority of his spare time with Monique.

Mid afternoon on a Sunday the phone rang it was doctor Kramer.

'I think the time has come to introduce Andrew into the real world, I think he is ready. He is a Class A student and in my opinion quite capable to transfer to a regular High School. That's if you agree.

'I will of course continually monitor his progress and if any problems occur he will return to my clinic immediately.'

'Lets get together with Andrew and see what he thinks' said Sam

Andrew loved the idea of attending a regular school and living with Sam on the 'Jon Jo'.

It was agreed that he would attend Heatherlands High in North Santa Barbara starting the Easter term after Christmas.

Doctor Kramer left to arrange the transfer from his special school to Heatherlands High.

Sam looked at Andrew and said 'I've been thinking very hard about what you said about being a family and I like the idea, but first things first, I want to adopt you as a son and not just as a guardian, what do you say?'

'I've been wanting that for such a long time, it would be so wonderful to have a dad' said Andrew.

Andrew ran towards his new dad and they embraced in a huge hug, each of them crying with happiness.

As soon as Sam arrived at the boat he got straight on to the phone and called Doctor Jon,

'Hello Doctor Li's residence,' answered Manuel

'Is the Doctor in this evening Manuel?'

'Hi colonel Sam, momento,'

'Hi Sam, Jon here, how are you doing stranger,'

I'm doing ok but need to see you, are you available tonight?'

'Yep, taking a night off,' said Doctor Jon.

'I'll be 20 minutes,'

Sam arrived at Jon's spacious villa with a firm handshake from his friend and a very dry marti*ni*.

'So why the urgency Sam,'

'Two things, one I need your blessing and two, I would like very much to marry your baby sister,'

'The answer is yes and yes, she will be so happy she has been in love with you since she was 16 years old, it would be a proud day for me to be part of the Lassiter family,' said Jon

'Thanks Jon, just one more thing I need her ring size, can you help?'

'No problem, hold on a second, as Jon went to Monique's room and picked up one of her dress rings.

'There you go Sam, go buy a nice ring,' said Doctor Jon.

The next morning Sam called at the leading jewellers shop in Santa Barbara and chose a ring with a huge diamond surrounded by two smaller ones, it was beautiful.

He then phoned Monique and arranged to take her out to dinner at Filippo's that evening.

'Is this a no date dinner,' said Monique laughing,

'You got that wrong "Spud" this is a proper date, I'll call for you at 8pm.' said Sam.

The restaurant was not very busy and the soft Italian love songs on the tape seemed louder than usual.

After the main course and half way through the desert, and two martini's later Sam produced the little ring box and laid it out in front of Monique. As she opened the little box Sam didn't say anything, Monique amid floods of tears said,

'Yes, Yes, Yes. I would love to marry you Colonel Sam,'

CHAPTER 58

Six weeks later on a beautiful early summers day Sam and Monique were married at the Santa Barbara registry Office, in front of a small congregation of friends and family. After the service and photo's were taken the party adjourned to Doctor Jon's palacial villa for a further blessing, speeches and reception. One hundred guests the majoratory high flyer's in the movie and fashion world moved around the lovely grounds and engaging in conversation.

The speeches then followed, everybody wishing the couple a long and loving relationship. The two Doctor's Li and Kramer said a few words and Sharon Clark delivered a lovely speech. Sam was a little worried when the Best Man rose to his feet and went to the microphone

'Ladies and Gentlemen I'm not really big enough to be Best Man, so I can introduce myself as Best Junior Adult, said Andrew.

I really hope that Monique and Sam have a long and happy life together and that they are as happy as I am, because as from yesterday my name is Andrew Lassiter and these lovely two people are now my new Mum and Dad. There is nothing in the world that could make me more happy than I am now. Ladies and Gentlemen , please raise your glasses to Mr. and Mrs. Lassiter, my Mum and Dad.' Andrew sat down to a tremendous round of applause, Sam and his new bride embraced the lad in a three way hug,

When the guests departed and Andy was safely tucked up in bed, Sam and Monique strolled locked together in the lovely gardens of Jon's villa.

'I have had to wait twenty years to be with the love of my life and I will love you forever Colonel Sam,'

Sam looked at his beautiful bride and said,

'I'm the luckiest person in the world "Spud".

Lightning Source UK Ltd.
Milton Keynes UK
UKOW01f1043040117
291311UK00001B/28/P